LASSO

Dick

Keith Publications, LLC
www.keithpublications.com
©2012

Arizona
USA

For Gene —

Thank you and All best wishes.

Cheers,

LASSO THE MOON

Copyright© 2012

By Dick Sheffield

Edited by Ray Dyson
www.raydyson.com

Cover art by Elisa Elaine Luevanos
www.ladymaverick81.com

Cover art Keith Publications, LLC © 2012
www.keithpublications.com

ISBN: 978-1-936372-63-8

All rights reserved.
No part of this book may be reproduced or transmitted in any form without written permission from Keith Publications, except by a reviewer who may quote brief passages for review purposes, with proper credit given.

This book is a work of fiction and any resemblance to any person, living or dead, any place, events or occurrences, is purely coincidental. The characters and story lines are created from the author's imagination or are used fictitiously, except for incidental references to public figures, well-known products and geographical locations, which are used fictitiously with no intent to disparage their products or services.

Keith Publications strives to release completely edited and polished material. Our manuscripts go through extensive revisions between our editors and the author. However, in the event the author feels as though the integrity of their writing has been jeopardized by edits, it is left to the sole discretion of that author to keep his/her manuscript as is. Any errors; grammatical, structural, use of Brand Names/Trademarked products and or historical are that of the authors.

If you are interested in purchasing more works of this nature, please stop by
www.wickedinkpress.com and www.dinkwell.com

Contact information: info@keithpublications.com
Visit us at: www.keithpublications.com

Printed in The United States of America

Dedication

To the memory of my mother and father

Acknowledgements

"What lies behind us and what lies before us are tiny matters compared to what lies within us."

Ralph Waldo Emerson

These words were sent to me by a friend once upon a time and perhaps sum up William Scott Bradford's journey in Lasso The Moon best of all.

I would like to extend my gratitude to Ms. Eudora Welty of Jackson, Mississippi, whose gardens were an inspiration, as well as to the many other gardeners and their blooming friends. Thanks also to the professionals who answered my original letter regarding the second ball.

And lastly, a special thank you to my wife, family and friends for their encouragement and support and to you–the reader–for undertaking this journey with William, Maggie and Jane.

Preface

CREED OF THE AMATEUR

Amateurism, after all, must be the backbone of all sport, golf or otherwise. In my mind an amateur is one who competes in a sport for the joy of playing, for the companionship it affords, for the health-giving exercise, and for relaxation from more serious matters. As a part of this lighthearted approach to the game, he accepts cheerfully all adverse breaks, is considerate of his opponent, plays the game fairly and squarely in accordance with its rules, maintains self control, and strives to do his best, not in order to win, but rather as a test of his own skill and ability. These are his only interests, and, in them, material considerations have no part. The returns which amateur sport will bring to those who play it in this spirit are greater than those any money can possibly buy.

Richard B. Tufts
Pinehurst

I want to see you game, boys, I want to see you brave and manly, and I also want to see you gentle and tender. Be practical as well as generous in your ideals. Keep your eyes on the stars and keep your feet on the ground. Courage, hard work, self-mastery, and intelligent effort are all essential to successful life. Character, in the long run, is the decisive factor in the life of an individual and of nations all.

Theodore Roosevelt
Book *Youth*

Book One

"Nobody looks for the moon in the afternoon, and this is the moment when it would most require our attention, since its existence is still in doubt."

Italo Calvino
Italian Writer

"Despite the bleakness and the desperation, there lives an odd optimism, that is, the chance to prevail."

John Cheever
American Writer

"Our great and glorious masterpiece is to live appropriately."

Michel de Montaigne
French Philosopher

"No man's knowledge goes beyond his experience."

John Locke
English Philosopher and Physician

1

William Scott Bradford loved the game of golf and pursued it vigorously from the primary angles of expectation and purity, two fatal flaws. His search for excellence and complete understanding in a sport that yields at best only possibility and uncertainty, left him charmed, baffled and on occasion, flat-out bewildered. It robbed him of time and granted him joy.

He first swung a golf club at the tender age of six, encouraged to do so by his grandfather, a talented and resourceful player in his own right. Many years had passed since that summer in 1954 when the old man began teaching his only grandson about the techniques, rules, strategies, and challenges surrounding the game. The exacting tutelage took place at the practice facility of his local club nearly every day that summer, mostly from the perspective of a small aluminum stool that stationed him at eye level with his young student. "Hit it hard," he said. "We can always teach you to send it in the proper direction."

But perhaps more importantly and without fail, the old man worked two basic tenets into every session. Each, William now thought, transcended the sport.

"Respect the game, your opponent, and yourself enough to give it your all," he said, regarding each shot. "And learn to have fun doing so, because if you cannot do that, you may as well climb another tree."

Those were seamless days, time well spent. As were the occasions when he visited his grandfather's library, where hundreds and hundreds of books lined shelves that ran from the floor to the ceiling. It was a warm room, complete with a stone fireplace and a constant stack of mesquite nearby. Two leather winged-back chairs with matching ottomans, an oak writing table, and a window that provided passage for the morning light and framed a flower garden just outside promoted a sense of privacy and peace. It became a place where the young boy's imagination believed anything was within reach.

A balanced mix of paintings and photographs decorated the walls, two of which intrigued William. One of Ben Hogan hitting his famous one-iron shot in the final round of the 1950 United States Open at Merion. The other was of a tall and slender young woman, with thick auburn hair and a face full of freckles, making her final movements through the ball. "Best swing I've ever seen," the old man said, telling the boy of the time he watched her and Hogan play an exhibition match at the Colonial National course in Fort Worth. "The truth is—I'm not the only one who thought so either." Her name was Maggie O'Connor, and she had a presence that haunted William from the first time he saw her.

William was forty-four years old when he moved back to Texas. After graduating with honors from two top-flight universities on the West Coast, he joined the prestigious law firm of Ropes & Black in San Francisco, where he represented the legal interests of corporate clients and learned about the politics of making and saving them money. Within a decade, William had become the youngest partner in the firm's storied history, a skilled trial attorney and negotiator on a path that would make him a rich man. But despite his accomplishments and prospects of a bright future, the young lawyer made a surprising move—he took leave from the practice of law and returned to his small hometown of Star, Texas, a place he had left behind almost twenty-five years ago.

There, he lived alone in the safest place he had ever known—his grandfather's house on Jefferson Street. There also, William started to think about golf again. He did so with a blend of clarity and purpose, with a keen interest in learning more about the game that had meant so much to him as a young boy. It rained all day Friday, the day William sat down at his writing table in the library to pen the letter:

15 May
Star, Texas

Ms. Maggie O'Connor
General Delivery
Calahan, Texas 78836

Dear Ms. O'Connor:

First of all, thank you for your time and consideration.

Like many others, I am challenged and humbled by the game of golf. My grandfather, a student of the game and I might add—your swing—taught me to play.

There are so many essential components to playing well, but whether one is a professional or an amateur, an accomplished player or an absolute hacker—everyone has struck a shot they would prefer to have back. And how often after this has occurred and when we are allowed, do we immediately drop another ball to the ground and make a stroke that more closely cooperates with our original expectations?

Ms. O'Connor, my goal is twofold: to learn how to play and understand the game at the highest level of my ability, and, to qualify for our state's premiere amateur tournament next year.

I would like to request your help in the effort, hence the note and my question, one the more I think about—the more open-ended it becomes: What do you believe are the keys to hitting the second ball first?

Again, my appreciation and best regards.

Sincerely,

William Scott Bradford
810 Jefferson Street
Star, Texas 79830

William signed his name to the letter and mailed it late the same afternoon. Naturally, before doing so, he read his words carefully, because he desperately wanted to state his case in a halfway intelligent manner. One part of him–his heart–signaled there was nothing wrong with sending the letter he had written, even if the person on the other end was a total stranger; the words were honest. But his practical side argued just as vigorously that he was acting like an absolute fool imposing himself on someone, especially if that someone was a complete stranger. William could not deny the apprehension he felt when the envelope left his hand and slipped through the mail slot to begin its journey. He held no expectations.
"Don't play it safe," he thought, as he left the post office. "It may not work out, but to hell with playing it safe."

To William's surprise, her reply arrived a few weeks later.

Maggie Justine O'Connor
P.O. Box 9227
Calahan, Texas 78836
June 2

Mr. William Scott Bradford
810 Jefferson Street
Star, TX 79830

Dear Mr. Bradford:

The quick and possibly flip answer to the question posed in your recent letter is to not commit the same mistakes you made when you hit the first one. But you asked a serious question, one that almost sneaked past me at first glance, and I will do my best to briefly address it.

I can think of many golf shots, in tournaments and elsewhere that I would have enjoyed hitting again. Of course I did not have that luxury, but during those rare rounds when a second ball was permitted, the outcomes were often more successful and equally mystifying. My father called this stroke Alfred. Why he named it that I will never know, but he simply said, "Alfred has never missed a shot. He is the best player in the world and cannot be beaten." My father was correct about most things.

William, golf is not a game of perfection. It is a game of possibility rather than certainty. Even a bad swing, grip, club fit, or poor lie will produce the occasional good, even great shot. On the other hand, the world's best players hit the occasional bad shot. Walter Hagen said he expected to hit at least two terrible shots in every round he played, and accepting that, he didn't let the bad shots upset him, whenever they occurred.

There is this possibility too: After we purge ourselves of the bad stroke and drop the second ball, we often hit it with (for lack of a better term)–mindless abandon; we let it go. We already know what can happen, so we strike the subsequent ball knowing that at the very worst—we'll hit it as poorly as we did the first one. Under those circumstances, what's to lose, right?

In my view here is the rub—a player can never hit the second ball first because the conditions have changed prior to striking it, and conditions determine play. The player has more information and less fear, therefore it is like picking the lotto numbers on Sunday morning. Now, the keys to not missing the first one—that is an entirely different matter.

I don't know if this helps you, but you asked and I replied, and I guess that's a square deal.
Good luck with your game, and thanks for thinking of me.
Best wishes,

Maggie J. O'Connor
LPGA Master Professional

William studied the contents of the letter several times before setting it aside. The words were well drawn, thoughtful and wise; a mixture of honesty and experience. They were spiked with humor, sensibility, and seriousness. She had understood the nature of the question, and driven a shaft directly into the heart of it with her answer—it was about the first ball. She had delivered a gift, one more precious than he had bargained for.

Although delighted by her response, William did not leave things there. He wrote a second letter, inquiring about the possibility of meeting in person. A few weeks later her reply set forth the details. Their first session took place in mid-September and lasted more than five hours. And its tenor and content varied from what William had anticipated.

3

William pulled his car into the drive of the handsome two-story home and followed it to the side of the house, where he parked behind a late model Ford pickup and a 1958 black Thunderbird. When he first saw her, she was hitting golf balls off a mat on the patio into a fairway that bordered the rear section of her property. A dense wilderness area, natural and untouched by design, stood off to her right, the closest neighbor about one-half mile down the road to the left. She had been a resident member of Fairway Farms since her days on tour, and its location provided the radical-type privacy she desired. It was six-thirty, a cool day under the sun, and the sound of the club hitting the ball solidly pierced the early morning silence–shot after shot.

Dressed in pleated camel-colored trousers, a black cotton turtleneck and black shoes, she was taller and leaner than William figured, but an absolutely striking woman. Although seventy, her auburn hair remained thick and wiry, with only a hint of gray. Her face was almost wrinkle-free, yet it was a face that had spent considerable time outdoors. She wore a pair of silver earrings and a simple bracelet on her left wrist. Her eyes were hazel, with slivers of green and gold in them.

"Sit down," she said, motioning to one of the Adirondack chairs nearby. "I'll be done in a minute. I like that you're on time."

The fifty balls she hit with a seven iron every morning traveled in the vicinity of one hundred thirty yards. Each ball assumed a near perfect trajectory as it left the ground, cutting through space toward its intended target in a slightly right-to-left pattern. She held her finish until the ball landed softly and stopped in the fairway grass. The swing remained crisp, perhaps more compact than in days past, but it did not possess an ounce of wasted motion, only a combination of ease, rhythm and balance few players master in a lifetime.

"There, all done," she said, before turning and extending her hand in William's direction. "Maggie O'Connor."

"Pleasure," he said, shaking her hand. "Thanks for seeing me."

"Why me?" she asked, taking her seat.

William handed her the framed photograph inherited from his grandfather and told her the story behind it. He then mentioned his specific goal regarding the Texas State Amateur Championship, but said he simply wanted to give his talent the opportunity to do its best.

"Do you believe you have talent?" Maggie asked.

"Some, but I would like to find out the truth and not fear failure or success, regardless of the outcome."

"Here, let me watch you hit a few shots," she said, handing him the seven iron.

During the next hour, Maggie asked the amateur player to hit about ten full shots with the club. She then handed him a pitching wedge and told him to hit the first ball fifty yards and the next five in ten-yard increments, up to one hundred yards. Then she asked him to repeat the drill in the reverse. Later, they walked to a nearby practice green and beneath her watchful eye William chipped, pitched and putted from short distances.

"Okay, that's enough," she said. "Let's gather up these balls and have a talk on the porch." They did so in dead silence before finally taking their seats.

"What do you do in real life?" she asked.

"I'm a trial lawyer."

"That's it?"

"Well, no. I've been working and living in California for more than twenty years and only recently moved back to Texas."

"Why?"

"I'm not sure."

"Sounds like a pretty significant change of pace—to suddenly uproot your life for no particular reason."

"Maybe to some, but I can honestly say it wasn't an impulsive decision."

"Are you married? Have kids?"

"No on both counts."

"About this change of direction—is it that you cannot say or will not say?"
"I'm not sure, really."

"You've asked that I help you with something and it is an effort that will require considerable commitment on both of our parts. I just think I'd like to know the motivation involved here."

"I really don't have an answer."

"Then, counselor, I'm not sure I can help you."

After a brief silence William told her there was something missing in his life and although he could not pinpoint it, he knew he had to come to grips with it.

"Everything was going great guns professionally, economically and in almost every other way, and then I woke up one morning wondering about the narrow path I had been traveling. That's it. No dramatic moment or news flash—just a void I could not escape, and unlike the flu or a bad cold, it would not go away.

"Honestly, and I feel guilty about this, I think I'd like to be happier."

"Why golf? Why turn your attention in that direction?"

"There is no guarantee, of course, but I decided to go back to a time and place where I may have been the happiest; and the most grounded. I have the luxury of being able to take some time away and well, this is what I've chosen to do. Some people might go to the beach or travel, perhaps drink too much whiskey–I don't know. But this is what I believe is right for me, at least for now."

"Look," Maggie said, "it's obvious you are a bright young man and I'm still uncertain why you have chosen me and golf, especially tournament golf, to flesh out this place in your life. Why not just whittle on a piece of wood or use the time in a fashion that would not require so much labor and attention?"

"I don't know what to say about that except that I want to push the limits of my ability in another direction, regardless of the uncertainty. I'd like you to help me on the golf side, nothing more. I'm really not sure what I am going to find out about myself or if it is even the right way to go about it, but I have chosen this goal to ride toward in the short term, and I am committed to seeing it through."

"Okay then," she said, looking him squarely in the eyes.

Maggie spoke candidly. She told him she admired and encouraged people who dared to dream and improve their lives. But she also said, "Talk is a cheap thrill–nothing more" and added the difference between visions realized and those not, often lie in the willingness or unwillingness to act upon those beliefs. She told him she thought people learned best through practice, whether it is golf, writing, dance, living or anything else–the principles were the same. She told him there would be no way to achieve his stated goals without practice.

"The game is difficult and fickle, no matter how hard you work." she said. "Every player must strike a fragile peace with it, because it will seldom proceed in the manner they envision.

"Ultimately, you must be able to teach yourself through the process of self-discovery, by learning to ask better questions–questions that do not always focus upon the results, but the reasons affecting the results."

She told him he must find the strength to remain positive against a wall of failure, and that he must learn to believe and expect to perform well, not merely hope to do so. She told him he must have faith in his efforts when things look bleak and to the contrary. She told him he must focus on what to do right rather than on what went wrong–that sometimes he must learn to simply let go and be willing to fail, then fail again. She told him, too, that he must always seek to fail better.

"Do you understand?" Maggie asked.

"Yes, I think so."

"Do you believe you can commit to this sort of internal effort and serve the type of apprenticeship that may be asked of you? Will you be able to trust my instruction?"

"Yes."

Maggie switched gears and said she wanted to ask about his convictions and beliefs. She did not care about knowing the answers, but suggested they might offer a glimpse of where he stood on some important matters. She told him it was not an exhaustive survey, but if answered thoughtfully, it might provoke more questions of his own.

"You will play your best with strong convictions," she said, handing William a list of printed questions.

What do you believe is more important, doing well or doing good?

Does character matter?

Does it wash over into everything we do?

Do you believe in free will or destiny?

Do you believe in God?

Do you believe less is more?

Do you believe will is part of talent?

Do you believe cheaters last?

Do you believe love matters?

Do you know what love is?

Do you believe the greatest happiness exists when you reach the mountaintop or during the climb?
What is the worst situation you can imagine?

Do you think the comment, "Look for the moon in the afternoon, because that is when its existence is most in doubt," has merit? Is it true or false?

"You see, the game of golf is best played from the heart and soul, because that is where our validation truly resides," Maggie said, as William studied the questions just given to him. "An accomplished player must be a good ball striker, but there is more to it than that– he must also be able to think, improvise and understand how to steady his performance when things do not go his way.

"Sleep on it and I will see you at seven-thirty in the morning, okay?"

"Okay," William said, heading for the door.

"Oh, and one last thing. Happiness may be the truest test of any choice–I give you high marks for pursuing it."

4

The pair agreed to several more sessions; the first slated a week prior to Thanksgiving, a second in January, and the final one set for the middle of March, approximately one month before the qualifying round for the Texas State Amateur Championship. All, particularly the one scheduled in late January, depended upon the weather. William asked permission to record the sessions and Maggie consented, on the condition the tapes not be heard by anyone except William until after her death. William also inquired about her fee, but she declined to discuss the matter and the subject was never brought up again.

"Where would you like to begin today, Ms. O'Connor?" William asked, the eagerness in his voice as crisp as the day. "Should I get my clubs and loosen up–what should I do?"

"You raise an important point, the right one at the appropriate moment. The answer is–I will always let you know what to do.

"One other thing, please call me Maggie, okay?"

"Yes ma'am."

With that simple exchange, the process had begun. That day, William never struck a ball with a club. She taught–her voice calm yet passionate as she spoke about the game she had studied and truly loved–and he listened, the new information flooding his mind. He recognized he had been fortunate enough to come to the right place, at the right time.

On the drive home late that afternoon, William drove past miles and miles of plowed farmland, the furrowed rows as fresh and endless as the thoughts in his mind. He listened to the strong voice on the tape and felt confident of the trail they were mapping together. A lot of work lay ahead and time would pass quickly, before he traveled this way again.

****

To Maggie O'Connor
3 October
Star, Texas

Dear Maggie,

Again, thank you for the time you spent with me last month. Your generosity and wisdom on the subject of golf and life surpassed my fondest dreams.

Also, I apologize for the lateness of this letter, but I've attempted to digest some of the things you asked me about before sending it off to you. Without question, I look forward to learning more about the game of golf each day–on the practice range here at my own club and certainly in the follow-up visits with you at Fairway Farms. But perhaps the boldest stroke made during those two days in September is the list of questions you handed to me. I know that you do not expect me to elaborate upon them in detail, but as they seem to dig into what I stand for–I'd like to say the mission is taking shape and appreciated.

My conversations about the human condition and about the basic ingredients of my own makeup have been few and far between for a longer period of time than I care to remember. Maybe it is one of the reasons I walked away from a career I had deemed so important and worked hard to build. Maybe doing well was not quite enough, right? I'm still thinking about that one.

I know my grandfather used to say, you can win the rat race, but at the end of the day you are still a rat–funny how that never quite registered with me before now.

Hope all is well with you.

Cheers,
William

****

To William Scott Bradford
Saturday, [Calahan, October 15]

Dear William,

Thank you for your recent letter. My approach to teaching is not for everyone, but it is what worked for me during these many years and I am pleased to pass it along to a willing and thoughtful student.

For any project there must be a sensible design. Think of it this way—Columbus did not just sail, he sailed west. Our path begins on the inside and works out. In my view, it is the only way to learn and fling oneself fearlessly into the world, regardless of the endeavor. Stay on path.

Wendell Berry, a Kentuckian and favorite writer of mine, once said, "It may be that when we no longer know what to do, we have come to our real work, and when we no longer know which way to go, we have begun our real journey." I take that to mean it is okay not to understand everything life tosses our way, and to embrace the difficulty that frequently presents itself to us.

Remember this: love, balance, time and place are the keys; they are part of the mystery in everything we do, despite the fact they may chuckle at us now and again.

Best,
Maggie J. O'Connor
LPGA Master Professional

****

He arrived around seven on an Indian summer morning in late November. There had not been a hard freeze yet, and the maples, oaks, and cottonwoods still held some of their color. William was excited about seeing Maggie again. She was sitting and reading in a large chair near one of her gardens when he approached. Although five minutes early, he somehow felt a half-hour late.

"Well, how have you been?"

"Fine," William said, taking a seat. "A little lost now and then, but I believe I've made progress. I hope you'll agree."

William then handed her the notebook he had maintained the past two months and sat quietly while Maggie thumbed through the details. The notes revealed he had missed only a handful of days of practice or play, and that most sessions ran about two and one-half hours, a healthy effort for an older, amateur player. They described the specific parts of the game he addressed on a particular day, the amount of time allotted them, any problems incurred or progress made, and some general comments. A separate section of the book broke down each round played and provided overall averages in several categories, including total score, fairways found from the tee, greens hit in regulation, number of putts, short-game saves, and bunker play.

"It looks to me like you certainly need to make more putts, and get the ball up and down more regularly, given the number of greens you are hitting in regulation," she said, glancing up from the notebook. "And if you improve upon your driving accuracy, I believe your approach shots will improve."

"I know it seems I pay for every misstep. It's frustrating and sometimes I wonder if I am ever going to learn to play this game to the level I believe I am capable."

She did not answer and they sat in silence awhile. He listened to the sounds of bobwhites, the rustling of leaves, and watched as a red-winged blackbird landed nearby and a large hawk soared through the air overhead.

"This place has always given me perspective," Maggie said. "Often our judgments ought to be placed in the proper perspective."

To Maggie O'Connor
13 December
Star, Texas

Dear Maggie,

This is a simple note of thanks, and best wishes for the Holiday season.

Winter has come to Star, but I practice when the cold temperatures allow. I have started a journal to write about the many layers of the game and sometime I stumble into parts unknown; some are connected and others are not.

Occasionally, I find a bit of clarity in that effort, but I soon lose my grip. I'd sure like to bottle those moments of transparency.

Your original list of questions still haunts me, but they too are coming into focus. I am attempting to shine some light onto them; however, I admit that many shadows remain.

All the best,

William

****

To William Scott Bradford
Friday, [Calahan, December 21]

Dear William,
Thank you for the kind words in your last letter. I also want to extend a fine holiday greeting and safe journey to you and yours.

As far as your golf game is concerned—keep working, because if you're not, someone else is. When I tended to rest on my laurels, I always kept in mind something handed down to me a long time ago, "If what you did yesterday still looks big to you, then you probably haven't done much, today."

I always enjoyed hitting balls in different conditions, whether it is the morning fog, a summer evening, or on a dark and dreary day. Practice, deliberate practice sets one apart.

But just as important is the notion of trust and faith in what you are doing. Patience is everything.

Best regards,

Maggie J. O'Connor
LPGA Master Professional

****

In the January sunshine, the pair met for a third time. She greeted him warmly, with a firm handshake and gentle smile. She looked thinner, especially in the face, but her eyes sparkled and her beauty remained. Once again she held court beside her flower garden.

"Have you ever been to the American Museum of Natural History in New York City?" Maggie asked.

"No, I've traveled to the city on business a few times, but I've never visited that particular museum. Why?"

"It's simply a wonderful place for the traveler," she told him. "You should go."

She described an exhibit of special interest—that of a beautiful wildflower garden and the effects thrust upon it by the different seasons. She told him what had captured her eye most were not the alterations that took place on the surface, but the perpetual activity beneath it by nature's many cast members. Maggie then pointed to her own iris garden nearby and said following the first freeze and into early March, many will see only a dormant and bare area.

"Nothing is further from the truth," she said.

She told William he, too, must wait for this movement to take shape; that he must combine the patience of someone injured or ill with the hope and confidence attached to progress and recovery.

"Maintain your focus on the process," she said. "Most importantly, remember what is often visible to others is not what contributes the most to our performance, either in golf or life."

"But in golf—maybe in other things, too—aren't we judged by results?"

"Perhaps. But like most things worth doing, the game ought to be played with a feel and thought that lie predominantly in your heart and mind. I will offer you some ideas on how to improve, however, the process of learning and doing is your responsibility.
"I can assure you that this will involve your mental, emotional and physical sensibilities and require patience, trust, acceptance and some mettle, among other things. Learning about them comes from experience, not advice. But take this to heart as well—do not accept what I say now, or anybody else says later, as gospel. There is no easy road.

"At times it may seem as if you are wandering around a dark room with a small flashlight, but there is joy in playing this game well and any player that seriously accepts the challenge, whether as a professional or amateur, understands that approaching the game in an uneven manner establishes a boundary for his talent that he will never pass beyond."

****

To Maggie O'Connor
31 January
Star, Texas

Dear Maggie,

My thanks have no fences to hold them nor do my words adequately describe how grateful I am to you for restoring my passions and replenishing my faith in life; in golf–all things really.

We have not spoken much about our personal lives; then again our conversations could hardly be more intimate. But one of the best parts of my life I sacrificed while working in San Francisco was the love of a woman named Jane Parker. Looking back, I was not even a good friend. She is a writer and lives in New York now, but we have been out of touch for several years.

I look forward to seeing you in March. By the way, happy birthday wishes next month–I looked it up.

Best regards,

William

****

To William Scott Bradford
Wednesday/Thursday, [Calahan, 10 February]

Dear William:

I think the actor, Bette Davis, once said, "Getting old ain't for sissies" and to a certain point I might agree. But given reasonable health, life is a state of mind. At any rate, thank you for the birthday thought.

Back to golf and your practice sessions. Golf is a complicated and unique game, especially for those that seek excellence. It requires concentration and tests not only our athletic skill, but challenges our courage, decision-making ability, and composure. That is why when practicing or playing, every shot must be considered as an integral part of the whole. To the extent you can focus your mind and free it from distraction, the better chance you will have of striking the shot you intended to play. Ultimately, that is all you can control – doing your part in executing the shot.

Your practice sessions must be viewed as a debt of honor between you and the game. The debt must be paid if you are to stay on that path. I suggest not leaving the course without making a specific arrangement when you will return. You have given your word, and there is no retracting it–that's the deal.

If you are incapable of this, find something else to do, because time is too precious and life is too short.

Fail better. See you in March.

Best wishes,

Maggie J. O'Connor
LPGA Master Professional

****

William reached Fairway Farms in the early afternoon on St. Patrick's Day for his last officially scheduled visit. Maggie wanted him to come later than normal, so they could talk some golf before sharing an early dinner. He was sitting in a chair by the garden, when he heard Maggie come out of the house. She wore all black and mirrored the brilliant day. The stars would be bright tonight.

"Hello."

"Hi, Maggie, looks like a good year for irises," William said, turning his head toward the choir of flowers, their huge purple and yellow faces straining for the sun's attention.

"They've bloomed earlier than usual. Pretty, aren't they?"

Her words that day turned to the competition William would enter next month. She did not alter her course or pull any punches when she advised her student that tournament golf required a competitive flame, and a burning desire that stoked it. She told him he must realize his best performance on any given day may not be good enough–that he might produce an excellent round, yet fall short of the mark.

"Accept the result, tip your hat to the victor and move on without regret," she said. "There is no failure in that–failing is not having the courage to send your absolute best out there. In this case, simply showing up is not quite good enough, at least in my opinion."

"Yes ma'am."

"By the way, whenever you are victorious, act like you've been there before."

Later, the pair walked a couple of holes and Maggie watched William closely as he hit the shots demanded of him. She zeroed in on his putting and suggested he concentrate primarily on hitting the ball squarely at the proper pace.

"Have you made a yardage book of your home course?" she asked, as they made their way back toward the house.

"No, not really. I've probably played it a thousand times since I was a kid."

"What about the course where you will play your qualifying round?"

"No."

"Do you know how far you hit every club in your bag?"

"I've never measured the exact distance I hit them, but I have a pretty good feel for that when I am on the course."

"It will help if you are able to trust your distances, especially on a course you have not played very often. Most importantly, you must know the rules. The rules govern play."

The conversation at dinner that evening centered on strategy and the rings around it–she focused upon the virtues of patience, acceptance, pressure, calm, experience, and the need to concentrate upon and commit to every single shot, regardless of the circumstances; things he had heard repeated on every visit to Fairway Farms. She told him again there was a world of difference between expecting to play well versus hoping to do so; that he must be aggressive in his execution, but to know when to take his medicine and play it safe, and when to take a chance. She told him to play the shots he had practiced, the ones in which he was the most confident and that would make the next play easier. Lastly, she told him to have fun with it all, and to let the game come to him.

"Hit it, find it, and hit it again," she said.

There was just the right mix between them. He left shortly after having coffee with her on the side porch, and for the first time, they embraced one another rather than shaking hands.

"Thank you, Maggie," William said, his heart and eyes full.
"My pleasure. You are more prepared than you think."

He did not know when he would sit beside Maggie's garden again– all he knew was he must do everything within his power to cultivate one of his own.

6

In late April, William arrived in Abilene a day prior to the qualifying tournament. He felt prepared, but anxious about his chances. Today, he planned to check his yardages, test the greens and determine his strategy in a practice round, before getting a good night's rest.

But when he returned to his hotel, a telegram and small, neatly wrapped package awaited him. William opened the envelope, and hoped the message was from Maggie.

Maggie O'Connor passed away today. STOP. I promised to get this to you ASAP. STOP. She spoke of you often. STOP.
Elizabeth Nathan
Laguna Beach, California

William was stunned; he didn't even know she was ill. He immediately phoned Maggie's home, but no one answered. He sat on the side of his bed and wondered what had happened. Sometime later, he decided to open the package he had been unconsciously tossing back and forth in his hands. Inside, he found the silver bracelet she always wore on her left wrist, and a note, written to him in longhand.

Dear William,
I wish you luck, you gave me joy.
Always,
Maggie J. O'Connor

Inscribed on the back of the bracelet in small block letters, were the words:
"Pass me a moonbeam, please"

Love always,
WPB

They were his grandfather's initials.

"Damn," William said, aloud. "They knew one another."

On the first tee the next morning, William stood behind the ball and surveyed the shot at hand. I must trust the work is done and let it fly–all the things Maggie taught me to do, he thought. With that, he embraced the uncertainty with certainty and struck a shot that sailed high down the right side of the fairway until it arched back to the left and settled softly in the perfect landing area. Walking toward his ball, he held the yardage book in his left hand and studied what lay ahead; all the while his right hand plunged deep into the side pocket of his trousers, finding and thumbing the smooth surface of the bracelet.

Book Two

"Trust yourself when all men doubt you, but make allowances for the doubting too."

>Rudyard Kipling
>Writer

*"Exhaust the little moment
Soon it dies.
And be it gash or gold
It will not come again in this identical disguise."*

>Gwendolyn Brooks
>American Poet

"There are all those early memories; one cannot get another set…"

>Willa Cather
>American Writer

"Only personal independence matters."

>Boris Pasternak
>Russian Poet/Author

1

The San Antonio Athletic Club was established in 1919, and since that time had been the site of more than two dozen state, national, and international championships; a fact not lost on William as he turned his car down the oak, pine and maple-bordered lane toward the famous clubhouse and courses beyond. As he moved further onto the grounds William slowed the car to a near crawl and lowered his window, his senses accepting at once the smells of freshly mowed grass, the sounds of songbirds, and the colors of landscaped flower gardens, not to mention the history and tradition of a place he had heard about since he was a boy. It was one of those unique moments—fleeting, yet branded into the memory; one, too, where his heart beat vigorously, child-like. Hardly any time had passed before he came to a gated checkpoint.

"Good day sir," the uniformed guard said, stepping toward the car.

"Morning."

"May I help you?"

"I'm here to play in the tournament. The name is William Scott Bradford."

The guard ran her finger down the list and found his name. She placed a check mark beside it with her yellow pencil and handed him a small red badge with black writing that read, *Contestant: Security and Parking Pass*.

"Just keep this on the left side of the dash for us," she said. "That way we will know who you are and can send you right on through."

"Oh, okay. That's it?"

"Yes sir. By the way, where's Star, Texas?"

"Out West, near San Angelo—about five hours from here."

"Good luck."

"Thanks, I'm sure I'll need it. Do you play?"

"Oh, no. It looks interesting, but three kids, two jobs—you know."

"Take care."

"Thanks," she said, returning to her post.

A few moments later William pulled the car into one of the designated parking spots near the clubhouse and switched off the ignition. He sat motionless and drew several deep breaths, his eyes cast toward the one word on the badge that stood out from all the rest—*Contestant*. His face cracked a half smile. It had been less than two months since he had won the qualifying tournament in Abilene.

It had also been that long since Maggie's death; a memory as fresh and distant as old love, and as delicate and warm as the grip of a small child. These two streams—one light and the other dark—unraveled an unpredictable joy and sadness inside him, and he fought to comprehend the strange unevenness of it all. It was mid-June, and the hot summer sun baked the land.

2

The memorial service for Maggie was held in the Willow Wild Cemetery on the outskirts of Calahan, Texas, no more than twenty minutes from her home at Fairway Farms. It was a simple and out of the way place located along County Road 17, bordered by perfectly cropped hedges and shaded with oaks draped with Spanish moss. A well-worn gravel lane wound by a small chapel and weaved its way past hundreds of stone markers—columns and plaques that had no uniform shape or arrangement, but stood perfectly still and erect in their random places, like soldiers at attention.

As he maneuvered the car slowly toward the gravesite, William heard the small rocks crackle beneath the tires. In the distance, several men raised a large green tent while another skillfully used a tractor and backhoe to carve a rectangular shape out of the earth, neatly piling the loose, red dirt he removed to one side.

At a bend in the lane, he stopped the car and got out. He knelt down on one knee in the grass that ran among the markers, and his eyes caught hold of a brown and yellow spider making an intricate web, perhaps a prison for the orange butterfly that floated on the breeze nearby; or a moth that evening. The markers were as varied as the lives they represented—flat ones and those with curves and carvings; shiny ones and dull-colored ones; those made of granite or some other type of stone; some gray, some white, some new, some weather beaten. Most neighborhoods were like that, he thought.

He read some of the names aloud, "Verna Ruth Howard, Jack 'Bud' Slaughter, Daphne Callaway, Raymond Frederick."

He looked closer—at the lettering that formed their names and the numbers that accompanied them. Most of the dates on the markers were separated by a single dash and centered below the name itself, but a few had the year of birth and death stacked vertically, one on top of the other. Those sets of numbers reflected time passing; of time spent and a life lived. Several of the markers had a brief description inscribed on them; great-grandmother, loving husband, teacher, and Capt., U.S. Army, among others.

But William wandered beyond those boundaries, and he wondered in what other ways and just how well these strangers he was now kneeling among had spent their time. He wondered, too, what had interceded to bring them here–illness, accident, war, murder, something else. He knew that to live life until the end was not a childish task.

"Are you kidding," he said softly, "it boils down to that dash, to those few years of opportunity?" If that were true, he wondered if everyone faced the same odds and obligations.

It dawned upon William what a personal place this was for some and not for others, and, how often in life shadows are cast between people. He thought how easy it is to never see or listen to these stories; to be completely unaware or indifferent to another's presence.
William sighed, and rose to his feet. Suddenly, he felt small and insignificant.

A few moments later, he again pulled the car to one side of the lane and got out. A fresh breeze touched his face and the morning sun moved just beyond tree level, its stalks of light sifting through the leaves and falling gently onto the mahogany casket below.

Like Maggie, the ceremony was private and to the point, and attended by less than a handful of others. Most of her colleagues had either passed on, were not in condition to travel, or simply lived too far away. Maggie would not have wanted the fuss anyway; she had always been protective of her privacy despite the fact she performed in public for many years. But that was long ago.

Other than William, Monsignor Patrick Sheridan, Elizabeth Nathan and two others attended the services. Elizabeth Nathan, an attorney and long-time friend had made the trip from California, and was the executor of the estate. Hector and Maria Ybarra may have known Maggie as well as anyone; for many years Hector had helped with the landscaping and outdoor chores at Fairway Farms while his wife Maria took care of the house and most of the meals.

"Hello Hector, Maria," William said, extending a hand to each of them. "I'm so sorry."

He had met the Ybarras briefly on his visits to Fairway Farms, but did not know much about them outside of their relationship with Maggie. As always, they greeted him with grace and humility, but could barely speak–the grief undisguised on their faces. The pair had raised eight children and all had received degrees from the University of Texas at Austin. Hector had worked two jobs his entire life–at the local feed store, and as a landscaper–to support the kids and give them a life through education he and Maria never had. They felt strongly about their responsibilities, especially to their children, and of course, toward Maggie. Maria was dressed in a simple black dress with a gold watch pinned to her chest, and matching flats. A black-laced scarf hung softly around her neck and shoulders. She was a small woman with short black hair and brown, intelligent eyes. Hector was tall and rangy, lean from the years of hard work. He had generous eyes, and a bushy salt and pepper mustache that stood out against his olive-brown skin. Maria held a crumpled white handkerchief, edged in black, in her hands, and Hector gripped the brim of his worn Stetson so strongly his knuckles ran white with tension.

"No good," Hector said.

"I know," William said, placing his hand on the man's shoulder. "Who is the woman speaking with the priest?"

"That is Elizabeth Nathan."

"Oh, she's the one that sent the telegram and Maggie's bracelet to me in Abilene."

"Yes. She lives out in California."

"Are you guys going to be okay?" William asked. They nodded, closed their eyes, and Maria pulled the scarf onto her head as Father Sheridan began the eulogy:

"What would the world be like if we all had the inner strength and integrity of Margaret Justine O'Connor?" the priest said. "It is, of course, an unknowable thing, but the odds are it would be a more interesting and perhaps happier place. Like each of us, she was a fragile soul, but also one that time and again reminded us that our humanity is a gift not to be squandered, compromised, or pawned for less than it is worth. She demanded that of herself, and expected it from those of us she knew and cared about.

"I remember one day in particular, sitting with her late in the afternoon beside her beloved flower gardens. I was a young priest, new to the parish at the time and she had invited me to her home for a glass of wine and personal introduction. It did not take me long to discover that I was also being checked out. We spoke that day and on many other occasions that followed about life, philosophy, politics, literature, and golf—you name it and at one time or another Maggie and I probably discussed it. Like most, I found her to be smart, wise, curious, passionate, completely honest, and blessed with a wicked sense of humor. She was an interesting human being, a compelling woman and a good friend. She was our friend.

"I remember that first day because during our discussion she offered up several ideas that helped to carry me through some difficult situations in the years ahead. They still do really, because they have such a universal appeal.

" 'Father,' she said, 'do you believe a human being can achieve anything near perfection in their life?'

"No, Maggie, I don't think perfection is possible—not for those of us on earth anyway. Do you?' I asked.

" 'Well, I guess I would concede sustained perfection is not probable,' she said, looking as she always did, directly into my eyes. 'But it is how one looks at the idea of perfection that interests me—it's one's take on it that matters, don't you think?'

" 'Go on,' I said.

" 'There is an old saying and I do not know where I first heard it or where it came from, but I have carried it around with me for some time now. To me, it applies to those inevitable losses and disappointments one encounters in their life. You know them; we all know them—those events that impact the heart, and the core of your spirit; ones that we never fully forget.'

" 'What is it?' I asked.

" 'It is not what happens to us, but how we deal with what happens to us that makes the difference,' she said. 'To say it aloud is the easy part; to believe and feel it—to install it into our being and implement it into our every action is the difficult part.

" 'You see Father Sheridan, I have always believed in the idea of perfection—in life, love, golf, whatever it may be. I choose to believe that the thrill of life lies in those moments when one thinks they are within striking distance of it and that it is possible to get even closer. It is a positive movement rather than a negative one.

" 'To me,' she said, 'one ought to (she mentioned to me more than once she considered ought an ethical term rather than a religious one) challenge the limits of their imagination, not limit them; one ought to strive to live rather than exist and in doing so, find a way to focus upon what to do right rather than what they have done wrong. Ultimately Father,' she told me that day, 'I believe we must have the courage to be daring—that in the end we must attempt to fail better, without regret.'

"Of course it took me awhile to understand Maggie liked to tweak things, especially those in positions of authority, but I soon came to realize that I had encountered an idealistic soul; someone who responded to the call of her heartbeat, and the convictions embedded there. She truly believed that despite the setbacks, bumps and bruises certain to incur on such a journey, it was what made life worthwhile. To her an effortless life was a meaningless life. She had shaped the idea in such a manner (and she had a gift for this) that I knew an awful lot was expected of me.

"You see, Maggie had some rare qualities outside of her obvious physical abilities; she was confident and cunning and understood that the stamp one puts upon his life resided in the soul. She played golf that way and she lived life that way.

"She told me one day that she had not quite made up her mind if the soul was a tangible thing or not," Father Sheridan said, smiling softly and looking down, remembering.

" 'Some Japanese believe the soul lies just behind the belly button,' Maggie said.

" 'I've not heard that.' I said.

" 'Yeah, right there,' she said, placing her hand just below her abdomen. 'That is where the validation of life rests, that is where we begin as we make our way into the world.'

"Our friend had a remarkable disposition and constitution; she had an unswerving spirit that lived life in the present moment, with few regrets, and it was an approach that bothered those constantly flinching from the truth," Father Sheridan said.

"Maggie Justine O'Connor came to age in a world dominated by men, but she never gave or asked for an inch of advantage— certainly not on the golf course, and not in life, either. In the end, she enlarged the lives of those who had the good fortune to know her. She did not fear death because she believed it was how one lived that mattered. She was the essence of courage, beauty, decency, and independence, and I ask you, how can anyone not admire that? She was outspoken and opinionated, but most of all, Maggie was a woman that had a generous spirit; she was charming, a learner and possessed an intangible dignity. It was a life that truly counted."

William's eyes searched his surrounding during the tribute. They latched onto things he might not have noticed if he had not been required to be still, and pause. Hector and Maria stood beside one another; they stood tall and proud, humbled by grief, but filled with a grace the priest had just spoken about. Maria wrestled with her handkerchief and Hector steadied her with his right hand–strong, thick and rough, gentle–that rested lightly in the middle of her back. It was an odd moment to note the love and respect the two shared for one another. It was also a welcomed distraction.

Two squirrels scrambled along a limb of one of the oaks; they stopped, started, fidgeted, tails erect, and sat quietly as if they were invited to the proceedings. There were many bouquets of flowers–irises, camellias, hyacinths, day lilies, yellow roses, sunflowers and lilacs, among others. A simple stone bench sat beneath the sturdy oak. It would stand guard over her and welcome the visitors during the coming seasons.

Father Sheridan ended the service with lyrics from one of Maggie's favorite songs: *"When I pass a rose and press the petal to my nose, I'll think of you,"* and then said, "Maggie Justine O'Connor–woman, citizen, and dear friend–I believe we all will.

"Thank you and amen."

"Amen," everyone said, together.

William glanced down at his watch and wandered over to Hector and Maria to say goodbye. The ceremony had lasted less than a half hour, but he guessed Maggie had it right–it is how one lives that counts.

"What will happen to you all, and the house?" he asked.

"Elizabeth Nathan said they will not sell the place, that Maggie made arrangements for us to continue to take care of it. We are honored to do so," Maria said.

"Good," William said, not realizing what part he might play. "If you ever need me for anything, anything at all–here is how to reach me. Star is not that far away."

"Thank you," they said, in unison. He watched them walk away–Hector in a brown suit, cowboy boots, hat in hand, and Maria in her simple black dress. Suddenly, the pair stopped and Maria bent down and picked up something from the gravel lane. She rose and opened her palm to show Hector two pennies that lay flat in her hand. The couple, he suspected, were in their mid-sixties and little things still mattered to them. In a good way, he envied them. Hector put on his hat and they moved away, together. William then turned, and waited for Elizabeth Nathan to emerge from her conversation with the priest.

"Ms. Nathan," he said, walking over to where she was standing.

"Yes."

"Pardon me for interrupting, but my name is William Bradford."

"Hello," she said, taking his hand. "I'd hoped that you would come."

"Wild horses could not have kept me away," he said, smiling nervously. "Knowing her, even briefly, meant so much to me."

"I know."

Elizabeth Nathan glanced over to Father Sheridan as he began to walk toward his car.

"Father, do you have a second—I'd like for you to meet someone."
"Certainly," the priest said.

"Monsignor Patrick Sheridan, this is William Bradford."

"William," the priest said, taking his hand.

"Father, thank you for putting into words what we all thought of Maggie."

"It was pretty easy. She was a remarkable woman."

"I'm headed to the house, would you care to join me?" Elizabeth Nathan asked.

"Sure, I'd be delighted," William said. "I'll be along shortly."

"See you then," she said.

"Pleasure meeting you, Father," William said.

William stood there for a moment and watched the pair disappear into Father Sheridan's black Lincoln Town car and drive away. He then went over to his own car to retrieve a wrapped gift he had brought for Maggie before heading toward the bench beneath the oak tree. This death business is like Hector said–no good, he thought, taking his seat. He put his gift to one side and leaned forward, his elbows resting on his thighs, his hands hanging loosely between his knees.

"Well, Maggie, I qualified for the Texas Amateur Championship in case you did not know," William said aloud, on a light note. "It will be held at the San Antonio Athletic Club in June, but my guess is you already found a way to keep tabs on me, since for as long as I have known you, you have managed, without much effort, to be about three or four steps ahead of me. Of course, without your help I had no chance to make the tournament, and I'd like to thank you with all my heart for that fact. You walked every step with me during the qualifying round in Abilene. Like you told me the first day we met–reaching a particular golf goal will never change who I am. It has nothing to do with anything really, right? Matter of fact the golf thing feels pretty insignificant at the moment, although you would tell me in no uncertain terms to stop being sentimental and pay attention."

"Believe in yourself and play that way," Maggie had said.

"But you know what–I believe you were more of a sap than you let on; that is what I believe. There is a large hole in my heart right now and I wonder how people find the courage and wherewithal to deal with such sadness. Our paths crossed and I am grateful–forever grateful.

"The bracelet you gave me was a complete surprise–not for the actual gift itself, but because of the connection it established with my grandfather. I am not certain if I need to know or want to discover what you two shared together, but I appreciate you trusting me with the truth. You always said that the truth works and is easier to remember–I believe that. In celebration of you, my grandfather, and the time we shared I've brought you a small gift. Perhaps it will shrink the distance between the three of us; I know he wrote on the back of the bracelet the phrase, *Pass me a moonbeam, please,* and I do not know if you had an answer or not; maybe it implied a secret message between just the two of you. Just in case and maybe for my benefit than any other, I decided to provide my own response: *I only have delphiniums.*

"The flowers are tall, lean, and beautiful, like you, Maggie. And the deepest blue I have ever seen. Please accept them with my heartfelt thanks," he said, laying them softly onto the ground.

Leaving Maggie behind – the reality and finality of it all–was difficult. In a short period, she had become not only a teacher, but a good friend. Like Father Sheridan had said, she made almost everyone she met feel that way. It was a gift. William knew he would return to visit her often. He felt an obligation to do so; more importantly, he wanted to do so.

****

To Maggie O'Connor
28 April
From A Stone Bench

Emptiness and melancholy live inside of me today. I'm wondering how the idea of love and balance works at times like these, when one is lost and cannot scrape together the proper words or thoughts that might provide some clarity and order to the circumstances. Surely there are other challenging moments ahead of me, but I cannot imagine they will be any tougher than this one–it is sort of like trying to walk across Texas on your knees.

Often we hope for certain things in our lives, but in between, the world lies in wait for us. Then again you never believed that hope alone was a good strategy.

The older I get, the more those certainties become less certain. Isn't that odd–I thought it might work in the reverse. How foolish of me. I want to be a learner in life; I want to trust that doubt and grace can walk together, and that nothing is to be feared. I realize this take on life will be difficult and even confusing at times, but I do want to find the courage to stay on its path; to one day have it take shape.

Today at the memorial service your priest mentioned how you believed in the idea of serious daring and that choosing a journey of this sort demands time, attention, and perhaps the ultimate commitment. Commitment–that's an act, right? As for me, I do not believe I have tossed my hat into that particular ring yet nor have I exhibited the strength to reveal my soul in that manner, without guarantee. I would, however, be pleased to find the fortitude to fail better each and every day. Maybe this is what is required.

I still look at those original questions you handed me last year and know there is a pearl or two of wisdom buried there somewhere. Sometimes I think I am too literal for my own good, and that your basic intent was to simply encourage me to set sail, paw the stars, and find my own path toward the things that truly matter in life. Am I right?

Perhaps you were preparing me for days like this one; for situations where it is not what happens to us that matters the most, but how we respond to them. That will never go out of fashion. I pledge I will attempt to keep my head on straight, and fight to find the sunlight as often as I can. A photographer friend once told me that the last hour before sunset, where the light is almost mystical, is called gentle light. I will look for the gentle light, but with the recognition it will not present itself every day in my corner of the world. Life is a crooked road, right Maggie?

Of course I am rambling and whining far too much for your taste, but somehow I am trying in my own way to appropriately say hello without telling you goodbye. I am not prepared to do that today. Maybe a simple thank you will do.

I did not know that you enjoyed music since our conversations mostly pertained to golf, but I am thrilled that you do, even pleasantly surprised by the fact. I often wonder if we really know anyone that well. It was my shortcoming not to have noticed.

I have always thought that music has such positives; it has the potential to connect us and last in our souls. How is it I still know the words to songs that were popular when I was in high school or college, or better yet, continue to be uplifted and made lighter by them? Is it purely the memories they resurrect or are they permanently etched into our hearts and minds in some inexplicable way? How is it that certain books, music, films, paintings, and photographs possess such power, they can make us pause before carrying us magically away? Ah, the beauty of art. As usual, I have more questions than answers, but I am convinced those things enhance life, that they truly do matter.

Our songs are so strong, don't you think?

These days I mostly listen to jazz—Miles Davis, Thelonius Monk, Louis Armstrong, Duke Ellington and Ella Fitzgerald. There are others: John Coltrane, Coleman Hawkins, and Bill Evans. But my taste in music varies too; one of my favorites, along with a man called "The Boss" and another named Dylan, is a gravel-voiced songwriter and performer by the name of Tom Waits. Today, sitting on this stone bench in the late afternoon, a verse of his sticks inside of my head—do not ask me why, I guess it just hits the proper note. It goes: Let's "...toast to the old days and DiMaggio, too/To Drysdale, Mantle, Whitey Ford/And to you."

Goodbye dear friend.

****

Elizabeth Nathan greeted William back at Fairway Farms later that afternoon. She was striking—tall and slim, athletic-looking, and her expensively-cut chestnut hair framed a strong and smart-looking face. Rimless wire glasses protected her blue eyes.

She was a California native, an attorney, writer, and junior golf champion who chose family and the law rather than professional golf. She was Maggie's childhood friend. Both women had been taught the game of golf by Paul Runyan, first at Mission Valley in San Diego and later, at the Thunderbird Club in Palm Springs.

"I'm sorry I took so long," William said.

"I understand. She meant the world to me and it is hard to let go. I've been here for almost a week now—working my way through all sorts of papers and documents—and I still cannot quite believe it. I guess you expect some people to go on forever."

"You were friends?"

"Best friends since we were twelve or thirteen years old. We met playing junior golf one summer in San Diego, and hit it off from the start. It was a strong friendship that despite the gaps never faltered; the type when we saw one another again we picked right up where it left off. We were fortunate in that way."

"Yes you were. I've always heard you're lucky to make five true friends in life."

"I know I can count mine on one hand."

"I understand the house will remain as is for awhile," William said, changing the direction of the conversation.

"That's right."

"What then?"

"As trustee, I guess I will eventually have to determine what to do with the place, but I am nowhere near that decision at the moment. We've had the legal papers in order for some time and this is the way Maggie wanted it and this is the way it is going to be for the near term. Hector and Maria will look after the place as if Maggie were still alive."

"Well, if I can be of help to you in any way, please let me know."

"I appreciate that. Matter of fact, Maggie mentioned that to me. You made quite an impression upon her, and she is not easily impressed."

"Thank you."

The two spoke for more than an hour—about the law, San Francisco, Texas, golf, the memorial service and, of course, Maggie.

"Look, I've got to catch a plane back to California later tonight, and it is a two-hour drive to the airport. If you are ever anywhere near Laguna Beach, just let me know. We have plenty of room, several fine courses to play nearby, and our place looks out onto the ocean. Offer is always open."

"Sounds great," William said, handing her his phone and address information.

"She left several things for you and they are upstairs by her desk. They are inside the brown leather satchel."

Elizabeth Nathan then handed him the key to the house and told him "it, too, was a gift."

"I do not know what to say," William said.

"It is what Maggie wanted. She knew you had some unresolved things on your mind and figured Fairway Farms one of the best places on earth to work them out."

"What about Hector and Maria?"

"They know and are thrilled. Besides, you can help keep an eye on things—I'm not getting any younger," she said, taking his hand and telling him goodbye.

Suddenly, William was alone outside the house; he was neither trespasser nor visitor as he fingered the silver key in his possession. Because he had always met Maggie in the back section of the property that bordered the golf course, he had never carefully studied the front of her place until now. The white clapboard two-story home looked as if it belonged in the Deep South rather than Texas. It had many windows—all framed by black shutters—and a dark red roof that had two white-brick chimneys offset and extending skyward, like telescopes spiking the air. It had a spacious yard and tall shade trees, and a side porch. A simple door and small black mail box on the wall beside it guarded the entrance. He wondered what lay in wait as he climbed past the two gardenia bushes and up the several brick steps, sliding the used key into the lock of the door and turning the latch.

Once inside William felt the warm light of the afternoon sun on his face and glanced directly at the wooden staircase that led to a second floor; he imagined her desk being beyond them, somewhere.

Entering the living room he noticed the fresh-cut flowers, southern light, and a brick fireplace, with a polished oak mantle. There, too, he found two matching European vases with painted foxes on them, a variety of music boxes, and French doors that opened onto a side porch. The porch had a swing, several chairs, and plants in pots sprinkled around; it faced east toward the morning sun and two large magnolia trees, a lone stone bench and camellia garden. A gentle breeze made its way through the open doors and into the rooms downstairs.

He explored more of downstairs and studied what he believed to be original paintings on the walls, above the fireplace and elsewhere, and he noticed almost every room, especially the living and sitting rooms, had shelves of books; most rooms even had books stacked neatly on other surfaces. He wondered if this obvious love of reading and golf had somehow drawn Maggie and his grandfather together.

Walking slowly with his hands clasped behind his lower back, William surveyed the shelves, and occasionally pulled out some of the inhabitants that stood shoulder to shoulder from their resting places—*A Mutual Friend*, *To Kill A Mockingbird*, *Lonesome Dove*, *The Collected Poems of John Keats*, to name a few. There was what looked like a family Bible and several dictionaries in languages other than English.
The books came in a variety of sizes, shapes, conditions, and subjects—fiction, poetry, biographies, screenplays, philosophy, history, and large coffee table volumes. Books on athletics had their own section, many of which touched on teaching, coaching and instruction, but by no means were they limited to golf. Words written by notable coaches like Rockne, Bee, Lombardi and Wooden stood beside those in her profession—ones by Armour, Bell, Hogan and Penick, among others. There too, William uncovered the collections

of noted sportswriters, and the fiction of Bernard Malamud and Ring Lardner, Jr. The rows went on and on, almost to the ceiling in some cases; the dark wood, the texture and smells of the books took him to a good place. At the end of one row, he found an odd duck, *The History of Philosophy* by Will and Ariel Durant. William selected it and inside found an inscription to Maggie from another Texan:

It is about letting go and getting rid of the tension; Socrates and Plato spoke of it often.

Best,
Jack Burke Jr.

There was a small English writing desk in the corner of the living room. It, too, was oak, dark in color and had a flat surface where one could pen letters, pay monthly bills or go through the daily mail. The desk had three large drawers, with brass hardware and some cubby holes to stash things. He considered opening one of the drawers, but decided against it. Instead, he moved away and stood beside the window that looked out onto wooden bench under a maple tree. Several cardinals flitted about. "What day is it?" he asked.

Eventually, but with curiosity he climbed the stairs. Her bedroom was simple—full-size bed, dresser, a reading chair upholstered in a flowery type of cloth fabric and a writing desk in the corner beside a set of windows. As he made his way into the room he ran his fingers across the white chenille bedspread that had batches of red roses embroidered into it. He peeked into her walk-in closet and there, hanging neatly, he saw things he recognized, others he did not—the high-heeled shoes, pumps and flats, dresses, shawls and several beaded purses, the types of things he had not envisioned her wearing. He thought how foolish and shortsighted he had been, and as he turned to leave touched the shoulder of one of her dresses. It warmed him; saddened him; knotted him inside.

He made his way over to the desk. It was large enough for the manual typewriter that sat in the middle and a single stack of note papers to one side. A wooden desk chair, with armrests and four strong legs, stood in front. There was a two-shelf bookcase, flush against the wall, on the opposite side of the desk; on top sat several framed photographs of what must have been her mother and father, and other visitors to Fairway Farms during the years. He recognized the stone bench in several of the pictures and figured it must have been a favorite place to pose. On the expanse of wall space there were a number of other photographs and paintings; portraits in oil, photos snapped in Venice and Paris, on a fishing trip to the Pacific Northwest, and another of an unrecognized poet. There were two separate ones taken with an American president; John F. Kennedy, standing and smiling beside her, looked tan and fresh, handsome–like the country in which they lived.

An abstract and slightly absurd-looking drawing of what appeared to be his grandfather hung among them. The pictures were neatly mounted and thoughtfully arranged. A few black and white golf photographs were scattered among the collage, but did not stand out unless one studied the walls closely. It was easy to tell Maggie enjoyed this part of her home. Memories lived and remained alive here.

The brief sat upright in the desk chair when he first laid eyes upon it. It was classic looking–well-worn leather, workable brass buckles, shoulder strap, and the fact it had been repaired a few times added to its character. William picked it up and felt the weight of it before setting it back down, unopened.

To the right and within arm's length of the desk two tall and rectangular-shaped windows allowed for a clear view of the garden below, a piece of earth that stretched southward for at least a half-acre. Distinct sections and levels comprised the large garden along with several sitting areas and a series of individual gardens that ranged from perennials, roses and camellias to cutting flowers and wildflowers. It sloped gently away from the house toward a woodland garden at the furthest edge. A natural preserve lay just beyond.

"It's timeless," William said aloud, leaning his shoulder against the wall and looking out, his mind wandering merrily along.

On the bookshelf, William found bound copies of the Texas Farm Bulletin and several journals that detailed the layout designs of the beds; there were planting and blooming schedules, the names of seedsmen from Nebraska and several nurserymen from North Carolina and Texas; and photographs from all sorts of distances and angles—close-ups, from the bedroom window where he now stood, the balcony, even the rooftop. There, too, he read about plans to make roses part of the garden, especially climbing roses; they had names such as Silver Moon, Lady Banks, Fortune's Double Yellow, Mermaid, Safrano, and Tea Roses, all as unfamiliar to him as a roomful of strangers.

In the perennial bed he noticed another type of iris, bearded irises. These flowers were different from the ones where he and Maggie sat and talked on his previous visits to Fairway Farms. In bloom they were as gallant in their purple, yellow, and green costumes as their sisters on the other side.

Bulbs such as tulips, jonquils and lilies filled the upper gardens, according to the drawings and sketches in the journals. But there were added notes on her favorites and the bulb farm where she purchased them. "The blue Roman Hyacinth and the yellow daffodils produced the most glorious clumps and patches of color come bloom time," she wrote.

It was dark now, nearly ten o'clock, and William shut the journal before kicking off his boots and lying down on the bed to close his eyes. He neither pulled down the bedspread nor removed his clothes. Pleasantly surprised and dog tired, he drifted off to sleep.

5

"Mister William, are you all right?" she asked.

William opened his eyes slowly—in a squint, really—as the morning sunshine poured through the bedroom window. For an instant he did not know where he was. He turned his head and looked in the direction of the voice.

"Maria?"

"I found the door unlocked this morning, and did not know what to think. I declare, Mister William, I'm glad it was you and not someone else in this house."

"I'm sorry," he said, shifting his weight and getting off the bed. "Guess yesterday took more out of me than I realized."

"Would you like some coffee before breakfast?"

"I'll take a cup of coffee if you have some made, but please don't go to the trouble of breakfast. What time is it anyway?"

"Eight-thirty. Wash up and come on down. It's no trouble, Mister William. I think it is best to stay busy."

"Okay," he said, watching her walk away. "Maria, please call me William."

She turned and faced him. "William."

After eating and thanking Maria, William gathered the leather satchel and journals he had brought down to the kitchen, and made his way into the garden he had seen from the upstairs window the evening before. The morning sun drew out the many colors of the gardens and the songbirds were in full rehearsal; together they made the place feel like a sanctuary. Several robins danced and ran along the St. Augustine lawn; they cocked their heads and proudly displayed their red breasts before resuming their search for insects, earthworms, and snails. A mockingbird sang confidently to everyone from the branches of an oak tree nearby. William stood in the arbor, his eyes accepting the beauty, his heart the calm.

A white-seated trellis and some latticework separated the arbor and upper garden from the lower one, and from this higher ground he could see all the way to the end—to the woodland section and black wrought-iron gate that opened into the natural preserve beyond it. William walked past the pink camellias, bearded irises and day lilies, each lifting their heads toward the morning light, just as he felt the warmth of the sun upon his own face.

The lower garden had the feel of a circular basin and contained a series of beds for roses, cutting flowers and wildflowers, herbs and even a small vegetable garden. There were more climbing roses, too, like the American Beauty and Wild Rose. At the tip end of the lower garden and at the farthest point from the house stood Maggie's woodland garden where pines, some desert mesquite, pecans, dogwood and other hardwoods planted years before provided a distinct border. The small path leading into the ten-acre natural preserve beyond the woodland garden looked inviting; it was clear the land was allowed to grow wild, but not unheeded.

William settled into a chair beside the rose garden and unlatched the brass catches of the satchel. Inside he found several things, all neatly positioned. The typed pages of a thick letter lay on top:

To Master William Scott Bradford:

Betty Jameson, a colleague and friend of mine from our days on tour, once said, "Maggie, golf is like a love affair—if you take it seriously, it breaks your heart; if you don't it is not any fun."

BJ was a beautiful creature, fun-loving Texan, and an excellent player; she was also smart as a whip and I think her statement sums up my approach to most things in life, including golf. It might serve you well to keep that in mind as you read along. We met through letters and they are gifts of time and thought, the very essence of kindness. I thought we might somehow continue that pattern.

Inside of this well-traveled satchel are some items that have some age on them; others are newly created. I have dispensed some unsolicited advice, commented on things I believe are important, and allowed, with some discretion, you to peek into my own history. My suggestion is to take the information to heart, but with a grain of salt; definitely with a sense of humor and perspective. It is an old woman's take on things in ways that you might not have thought of or experienced–that is all.

By now my dear friend Elizabeth Nathan has given you the key to the house at Fairway Farms. I want you (no obligation of course) to come and go from here as much as you like; I spent many good days here–with family, friends, and solo–and my hope is that you too will find your own places to read, think, simply pass the day or perhaps find your way. Life is an interesting ride; one filled with mishaps and fine surprises. Learn or at least attempt to learn to treat those polar opposites the same. As always, that is up to you.

William, I want to keep this place alive–you only have one set of memories, you know. The gardens are a large part of that for me; they are filled with life lessons, calm, and joy. Perhaps there is no greater intimacy than between nature and human beings; there is certainly no greater teacher than nature, I think.

One fundamental request before I continue. Hector and Maria Ybarra are a big part of Fairway Farms and will remain so until life intervenes or they decide differently. I have seen to that, maybe in greater detail than any other. Be kind and respectful of them (I know you will), but make certain others are too. They have had a tough time of it. In their presence, my privacy was keyless and as time has worn on, they became my trusted friends. They took care of me through thick and thin–always. I'd like to believe I returned the favor. Luckily, I've learned a great deal from them. Are you prepared to be lucky–you should be, you know?

Let's take a walk around the grounds, shall we? Bear with me on this, because I believe it is important. Since our visits took place on the part of the property that faced the golf course and our time was spent almost exclusively upon the subject of golf, you have not seen parts unknown.

I'm bringing along an old friend–J. Rayburn Young–to offer her added take on matters. Although born in New York, she has lived on the Connecticut coast for the last forty years. She is a poet, writer, thinker, and swimmer in the ocean; and like any gardener, an optimist. I taught her about golf and she taught me about nature–plants, trees, flowers, herbs, and the sea, among other things.

The fact she wrote some of her poems and rhymes in this garden is a source of pride for me, but I could never claim the green thumb of her or her many friends who were able to get their blooming friends to do most anything they wanted.

"I do not see how you do it," Maggie said one day.

"What?" J. Rayburn Young asked.

"Present the flowers in such a way that I–well, view them as human beings."

"It's easy, they are living things. Nature is a marvelous teacher."

Let me provide you with some history about the gardens. They run from north to south, and were planned in the style of the day when I was a little girl. By that I mean they are distinguished by sections of like plants, with plenty of informal borders.

Maria will have fresh flowers and greenery in the house at all times–I like nothing better. The cut flowers, with their strong stalks and various flavors strive to last as long as they can. I like that they try so hard; it is an admirable quality. Depending upon the season, you will find that everything from poppies, hollyhocks, cosmos, zinnias and snapdragon, gardenias and lilacs make their way into the house and magically lift the spirit. Did you notice the vases with the painted foxes on them?

"Did you see the two vases with the hand-painted foxes on them," Maggie asked.

"Where did you get them?" J. Rayburn Young asked. "They're stunning."

"London. I was so nervous about shipping them back home."

"They're perfect. I especially like the fact both foxes are dressed in coat and tie—and holding the umbrella is absolutely the perfect touch."

William stretched his arms skyward, slightly shifting his body position in the chair. The morning sun warmed his face and he closed his eyes a few seconds before glancing toward the wildflower garden; somehow it looked different—more familiar. He returned to the letter.

I hope you will find the garden a pleasant place. The sights, sounds, observations, and surprises are all present if you will look for them. I say this because it is always a good idea to keep wonder alive, don't you think? There is a certain rhythm to a garden. Through the years, I have explored some of my greatest joys, and lowest moments here; I have found order, peace and quiet at times, but not always. It's that crooked line, imperfection thing I guess; human folly, too. Working here often took me away—I suppose I was thinking; maybe I was dreaming. And there were times where I believed I knew every inch of this place, but of course, that was not true. Things change.

There is plenty of beauty here, some of it more challenging to appreciate than other parts. It is sort of like comparing the Atlantic and Pacific Oceans: nothing is more immediately compelling than parts of the Pacific coastline, but the Atlantic—what a magnificent site that is. J. Rayburn Young showed it to me one summer when I visited her in Connecticut. If I recall, I had a shoulder injury that sidelined me one spring; it ultimately required surgery, then several months of rest before I could swing a club again.

"Where does the ferry go?" Maggie asked, driving the small car aboard.

"From Bridgeport to Orient Point," J. Rayburn Young said, pointing across the waters of the Long Island Sound to the east. "It's another hour or so to the cottage, once we arrive."

It gave me a chance to view a world different than my own. Provincial and comfortable is easy, but not necessarily the best, you know? Mostly, I believe we must fight endlessly for our comfort. Anyway, that particular day we boarded the ferry and crossed the waters of the Long Island Sound, traveling to her small cottage by the ocean in the village of Westhampton, New York. The cottage sat on what was an old potato farm; it had weather-beaten shingles, vegetation growing wild on every side, and fine windows we opened immediately upon our arrival. JRY believed it showed the world the cottage now had inhabitants, which it did. Once there, we walked the beaches, ate lobsters and corn on the cob, maneuvered our way around the weeded dunes, and felt the powerful presence of the Atlantic Ocean, which refused to be ignored.

It's those oceans I am thinking of when I asked: How do you compare a camellia to a cactus? Both have their own beauty, I guess that is my point–it is simply different.

Near the loblolly and black pines of the woodland garden, in a desert-like area, you can see the red and yellow blossoms atop the ears of the prickly pear cactus; there too you will find the hearty yucca, with its daggers shooting sideways. Inside of the fibers of its white blossoms lives a yellow and black Scott's Oriole. The pampas grasses, mesquites, and hearty scarlet and purple sages are pure West Texas, without the mineral rights of course.

Have you wandered about my place yet, or have I completely confused you? I don't mean to, because nothing I say or have said, or have done is on an industrial scale. This is my tiny piece of the world and now it belongs, in part, to you. My clues and riddles may remain a bit mysterious to you for awhile, especially in how it relates to your golf game (we'll get to that shortly, and I would ask that you not skip to the end). I know it must be slow going, following me around like this.

The gardens are a place to learn; they are a living photograph of change. Change does not have to be a bad thing you know; otherwise you might just end up where you are going. Have I said that to you? My apologies–it is not my intention to harp or preach about matters. Lord knows I've messed up plenty during my lifetime. Then again, our imperfections can be our most beautiful parts. I'm certain I'll get to that when we start discussing golf.

The gardens will also heighten your senses: the rain, the seasons, the crickets and locusts, the bellowing frogs from the marshes of the preserve; the birds, the colors, the sound of the wind, the crackling of the lightning. Not to mention the moon and the stars. If you are aware and pay attention, the rhythms and tempos of the garden–life lessons, golf lessons–are more affecting than their outward beauty. There is so much more. Let it seep into you, like you would the oxygen from the air. Be patient and enjoy the process.

You might notice that the stone paths, irregular and made of Austin stone, let you navigate around the place. They are good on a wet day, because our clay soil will stick to your shoes, but do not be afraid to take your shoes off and walk on the grass; or to lie on your back and look up into the blue sky; or peek into the corner of the Big Dipper at night. Have you looked for the moon in the afternoon yet?

I hope you watch the butterflies and how much they love the butterfly boxes Hector made for them. For me the hardware – the latticework, trellises and boxes–help to connect the dots. I love the benches and chairs scattered about; test them and find your favorite place. There is one.

"Let me take a photograph of you on the bench by the tree," J. Rayburn Young said, her neck craning to get the top of the pine included in the picture.

Maggie took her seat on the stone bench and removed her straw hat; she held the hat gently on her lap, part of its brim hanging just below her knee.

"These are not all pines?" J. Rayburn Young asked.

"Mostly, but not all. It has taken some time for the woodland garden to take shape, but now the trees hover over the lower garden; the pines and hardwoods are like a protector or something. But to answer your question–there are oaks, maples, dogwoods and ash here, too."

"What's beyond?" J. Rayburn Young asked.

"Those paths lead into the natural preserve. I got the idea when I visited the Hampstead Heath, outside of London. Anything goes out there."

"Did you go to the zoo or to Keats' house when you visited Hampstead?"

"No. I spent almost the entire day in the heath. I remember it was cold and rainy, muddy, and I saw almost no one the entire time, except for a group of circus performers that were camped along the edge of one side. It was a magical place to me. We had a short layover that day, before we took the train to Scotland for an exhibition match."

The gate at the edge of the woodland garden will lead you into the preserve. There, you will stumble onto things, and past things: things like the cane break, and the marshes with uneven stalks of reed and redwing blackbirds perched upon them, like centuries. I keep an old wooden boat on the banks of the marsh and have watched many forces of nature take shape from those planked seats during the years. Salvage this land–all things are eligible to roam in the preserve, like the democracy in which we live. I believe allowing it to exist in these terms makes it more beautiful and stronger, not the reverse.

William looked at the trees Maggie spoke about in her letter–their trunks, some curved and others straight as a string, reaching skyward. As his eyes scanned the pieces of the woodland garden, he took in a lofty and complex world of branches, leaves and needles–a world so remote from his own. The black gate that opened outward into the natural preserve was visible in the shadows, as was the narrow dirt path beyond. After a moment, he began reading again.

I have been hesitant to address the subject of your grandfather; we knew one another some years ago, and I've wrestled back and forth with the idea, since your first letter. Mainly, how much should I reveal? Because it is a private matter and I have always had difficulty releasing those parts of myself recklessly, I'll play it close to the vest for the moment. I hope you will trust and respect my judgment where this is concerned despite the fact I will give you access to some particular things. Some are far too precious not to pass along. Let me say one thing to you–this Jane Parker you mentioned in one of your letters–please do everything possible to make sure about her.

"Do you love him, Maggie?" J. Rayburn Young asked.

"I'm not certain I know what love means. I've been selfish, because I've had to–with trying to be an excellent player, teaching, fighting to establish my own life and all; then again, maybe that is an excuse rather than a reason.

"I even have an odd take on the idea of family. All of mine are gone now and for as long as I can remember, I've danced to my own heartbeat. Is that selfish–probably? I take full responsibility for my choices, and hope to never consciously shy away from the truth, but how does one judge such a matter? A golf career requires so much time and I have never found a stronger pull toward anything else. That's kind of sad, don't you think?"

"I'm not so sure–you have chosen to do positive things with your life, and there is a lot to be said for that," J. Rayburn Young said. "With risks, there are choices and consequences–it's that simple. Clearly, you are holding something back, and I wonder why?"

"For some reason, I fear being without options. I do hate that I have hurt him so."

William, you know what I think I like best about nature—at least my ideal of it: That at its core, there is an earnest sincerity; that it has the ability to treat the pressure of expectation and performance as fun; and that somehow—better than most human beings—follows through. I wish I were better at that part of life. Oh well, forget, focus, and forge on.

Knowing Maggie, this letter and the rest of the items in the satchel must be headed somewhere, William thought. His head swam upstream at the moment, searching for some clarity and understanding.

Inserted into the text of the letter was a single page that looked to be from a composition book or sketch pad. There were no dates on it. The small watercolor was done on a thicker bond of paper and had an imaginary black frame drawn around it; the verse was written in calligraphy, with black ink. Offset and to the right of the verse were three chives that ran the length of the paper, their long green stalks topped by pinkish-purple heads.

In the bottom left-hand corner of the page were again the familiar initials of his grandfather. The painting, entitled *Chives*, must have been a gift, but what did it accompany and under what circumstances? William imagined their discussions being about far more than swing technique or tournament results. Surely they spoke of love, travel, things that last and far outdistance the others we sometimes care too much about. There was no mistaking the watercolor was personal and like a letter, required time and effort. It looked as if it had been framed at one time or another.

William attempted to read some things into the poetry—scrambled eggs and chives—who talks about that sort of thing if they had not stayed the night, he thought. Had it ended badly between them? His mind moved more swiftly than his eyes.

"Do you love him," J. Rayburn Young asked again. *"It's sort of flattering that he gave you a watercolor with my rhyme on it. He had to spend some time finding it—my stuff is not exactly in every corner bookstore."*

"I've told him about you," Maggie said.

"He sounds too good to be true."

"I've decided I do not know anything about love."

Now to golf–bet you figured I would never get around to that subject. William, the first thing I'd like you to consider about golf, especially tournament golf is to have the courage and stamina to chase your potential; to be daring enough in your attempt to lasso the moon when others thought you could never get off the ground in the first place. If you choose to do so, you must understand and enjoy the process that surrounds the game–of practice and of knowing each shot, however struck, is an essential part of the whole.

What does that mean–in part, it is for you to figure out. For starters you must decide why you play the game, how deep your well of desire runs, and what you are willing to put on the line, without guarantee of comparable return. Idealistic–you bet it is. So is being an amateur player; if done right–it is the purest and strongest reason to play. If done right.

I dispensed some valuable information to you about the physical, mental, and emotional mechanics of golf during our sessions that began last year; you must practice them together and never separately, whether it is on the range or the tee on medal day. Remember to play the ball as it lies, to play the course as you find it, and when in doubt, always do what is fair.

Good luck to you.

Postscript:

As an afterthought, I decided to include in this letter/small manuscript my initial unedited attempt at answering your original question: "What are the keys to hitting the second ball first?" It was a freewheeling session late one night and I hope you consider it more humorous than anything, definitely different than the whittled down version of my reply. Before I forget to mention it–there is a second envelope in the brief. It should be opened only after the Texas State Amateur competition.

Finally this—although I have attempted to teach you some things about golf, I want you to understand that I never tried to stamp you in my image, only bring out certain qualities that already existed inside of you. It is a practice of mine to get as much out of the player as I can, not impose myself upon his or her game. This is all teaching is, because ultimately everyone has to determine their own way of doing things. My fondest hope is that one day you will leave the shallow end of the pool and swim in the ocean; that you will be willing to sail against the wind and with it too, if you are that fortunate. Please learn more about your spirit, soul, heartbeat, and the quirkiness and folly of the human condition. Appreciate what you have, and what is around you—the garden is a good teacher.

The rest, again, is for you to discover. Be earnest and industrious. Stay on path, have faith in yourself, especially when you have no reason to, and always fight to do your best, regardless of the circumstances. Fail better, if you know what I mean.

"William," she said, softly.

William looked up and saw Maria standing there. She had made a sandwich and pot of tea. "You're going to way too much trouble for me," he said. "I'm getting spoiled."

"Good," she said, pleased.

William took the small tray and set the papers aside. He decided then and there not to ask anyone about Maggie and his grandfather, despite his curiosity. He figured, in some way, she would tell him. After lunch, he reached into the leather brief and retrieved the remaining things Maggie had placed there: he found three books by J. Rayburn Young, a small homemade plant press, Maggie's United States Women's Amateur medal, and the second letter that would remain sealed until after the competition in June. He studied all of the contents before reading on.

Mr. William Scott Bradford
810 Jefferson Street
Star, TX 79830

Dear Mr. Bradford:

You may have gotten more than you bargained for here. I absolutely love your question, and it is one that any true hero or heroine of the great game of golf should answer in some shape or form; perhaps in a novel.

Some time ago, I cornered a colleague of mine after an exhibition match in Dallas and I asked him a question that went something like this: "Walter, on the occasions when I am playing and feeling good; when I'm in the zone and my aura is just right; when I hear the grass talking to me before I launch a shot completely outside of myself–I have to ask–where the heck does that come from?

"Walter," I said. "You study this kind of stuff–what do you think?"

He looked me straight in the eye and said, "Blood sugar." Then he reached into his suit pocket, pulled out a box of raisins and handed them to me. He just started laughing, but it was a straight answer to a BS question. Of course, Walter Hagen was the same man that once said about practice– "…practice, that requires discipline; I tried discipline once and did not like it." But despite his public persona, Hagen worked diligently at his game.

Golf by nature, is a game of first chances. The only percentage that counts is the percentage on the first try. One day, I set down my chalk line for a ten-foot downhill putt and hit enough of them where the ball went in time after time; it was if I was putting down a gutter. A local high school kid stood by and watched as I holed twenty or so in a row. He was amazed until I coaxed him over and he proceeded to make ten.

Part of golf's charm and frustration is the mixture of anxiety and expectation that accompanies every shot. Often, we "get in our own way" relative to shot preparation and rarely just let it go, free of distraction. The second ball then is really a counter shot to the first– one where the mind re-programs itself based upon the original results. Many sports have a similar situation–shooting free throws in basketball, pitching a baseball, first serves in tennis and so on.

In my opinion golf is a game of luck. Are you prepared to be lucky? I define luck as any event where too many scientific forces come together too quickly to calculate. For example, you hit a screaming hook into the trees from the teeing ground and the ball ricochets off three of them and bounces back into the fairway. That is luck. However, the ball was also bound by the laws of physics as it hit tree number one at a certain velocity and angle, deflected off tree two before striking tree number three and landing on one of twenty million blades of grass in the fairway. Luck has many potential components: Luck is the residue of design; luck is when preparation meets opportunity; luck is the more I practice, the luckier I get. There is a common thread here and of course, it is that luck follows previous and deliberate practice. I believe that.

Skill, in fact multiple skills, are inherent to the game. Driving the ball for accuracy and distance, playing iron shots onto the proper section of the green complex and controlling shots from bunkers, uneven lies, tall grasses and with the right trajectory into a stiff wind are just a few. And the most relevant of all golf shots may be putting; something that is probably more art than science and requires some courage to be successful. I could go on, but in sum there are many skills attached to the game and one is lucky to learn them.

A game I play when I am alone and working on my skill-level is a scramble. I hit three balls per shot and for nine holes I usually post a score of between twenty-nine and thirty-one. This drill is a great way to enhance skills on the course and learn that it is physically possible to shoot these types of scores. In this way the second (and third) ball is a tool to build success in the brain and is not a perversion of the game at all. So when you and God are paired together at twilight and you cannot break par, how are you going to do it for real? Hit until you are happy—why not?

Although the beauty of the second ball is that the heart and mind pay it less attention, it has no relevance in tournament play. In competition, the tour and amateur player must train to hit the second ball first by placing themselves in situations where every shot counts. In my view, the best ways to learn these technical, mental, emotional and spiritual aspects of the game are by concentrated practice and competition.

I remember when I was a young player—if I defeated Mildred (Babe) Didrikson Zaharias once, I beat her a thousand times on the seventy-second hole of the Open Championship. So—in your practice, pretend every shot struck is a second ball.

Another key element is to place your game in situations where the second ball is an impossibility; that means some form of competition. When there, be a Scotsman—hit and chase it as fast as you can.

There's a story that's been around for years about a young American playing in his first British Open at St. Andrews. When he arrived on the first tee he introduced himself to his playing partner, a veteran Scot. The American had the honors and after addressing his ball, took a practice swing in preparation for his shot.

"Laddie, what are you doing?" the Scot said.

"Taking a practice swing," the American said.

"Ah son, that's cheating," the Scot said. "Just hit it."

Postscript: I remembered a couple of things my former teacher used to tell me when it came to playing; he referred to them as the three cares.

Care-free: This occurs when the player is in the zone and playing well. No thoughts—simply see the shot and hit it—just meet the ball.

Care-ful: A player hits one erratic shot and suddenly he's yanked back into reality; his mind becomes a flooded state of bright colors that tie him into knots and destroy any successful swing possibly.

Care-less: A break through state of mind where the player develops an attitude of I couldn't care less where the shot goes. He aims his body in the stance, selects his club for shot value and decides to throw it into the air or at the hole as an offering to the golf gods. Let them direct the flight; he couldn't care less.

Lastly, and I've heard this piece of advice from my first day as a professional on tour—"the only way to learn to play on Sunday is to play on Sunday."

William sighed, and decided he would leave the second letter at Fairway Farms.

"How did she know I would make it?" he asked, aloud.

7

William entered the clubhouse of the San Antonio Athletic Club through heavy oak doors and found a main lobby that was well lighted, active, and striking in taste. To his left, a wide staircase led to a series of second-floor suites and private rooms for members and their guests, while to his right were various sitting areas and seating arrangements. Two fireplaces and traditional, dark furniture blended with the overall design and made it a room for all seasons. He noticed hot tea, hand-squeezed lemonade, and fresh pastries were served every afternoon at four.

Two informal dining and drinking establishments, the *Sullivan Grill* and *Oak Room*, along with several shops sat just beyond the registration desk; further down a maître d' stood guard at *The 1919*, a renowned restaurant known for its exquisite French food, steaks, wines, and service. He peeked into the formal dining room and admired the tall ceilings, and overall elegance. The place impressed him, even if this was not—as they say—his first rodeo.

To the rear of the main lobby and out two sets of French-style doors, an elevated porch ran nearly the length of the entire clubhouse, a distance that covered maybe forty yards. From there, beneath outdoor ceiling fans that swirled in silence he could see the configuration of the eighteenth hole, the place where the championship would conclude. From the teeing area between the hardwoods and pines more than four hundred and fifty yards away to the undulating, pear-shaped green directly in front of him, William imagined his spot among the footprints of others. In between, there were various types of bunkers, deep rough, and a fairway that ran uphill and made a slight curve to the right. He surveyed the design and wondered if it were possible for the entire layout to meet the beauty and standards of the final hole.

Little did he know how it would look from the teeing ground later that day, when all the players would see was the rooftop of the clubhouse, its twin chimney stacks, and a small, rectangular room located to their right. Later, he would discover that particular room was a studio apartment reserved for the club champion. Today, William felt every ounce the visitor. Although he had traveled some in his life, especially while living in San Francisco, this was a first-time encounter as a contestant in such a historic place. The fact his head was already spinning surprised him, and tugged at his confidence.

When he returned to the main lobby a smartly dressed woman introduced herself and directed him to the players' registration headquarters several doors away. There, tournament staffers greeted him cordially, asked him to sign the leather-bound scroll, and provided him with basic information and instructions–pairings, schedules, locker assignments and other amenities. His heartbeat quickened as he placed the key in the door of his second-floor room.

Later, as he moved toward the section of the clubhouse where the golf shop was located, William passed photographs that spoke in more detail to the history of the club; a time when oaks were newly planted and the greens were small and flat; a time when players wore starched shirts and ties, knickers, and competed with clubs made of hickory or ones with names seldom heard anymore. There were pictures of Ryder Cup teams, exhibitions, club champions, and one of Hogan when he won the United States Open in the early fifties. Touring professionals had always held memberships here, as did politicians, heads of industry, and other athletes and entertainers. The San Antonio Athletic Club had the reputation of choosing its members rather than the other way around. William soaked up the surroundings, but with reservation; he valued the manner in which this place upheld the tradition of a great sport, one worthy of attention. However, the photographs brought to mind the other side of the game's history too, one where walls–sometime invisible and at other times not–had excluded some who wanted to play, despite their talent and skill.

At the golf shop, he asked about his pairing for the practice round that afternoon, the location and hours of the practice facility, and where to find the office of the caddie master. He had not decided if he would carry his own bag, as was his custom, or let someone who knew the course far better help guide him along. He marveled at the large inventory of equipment and apparel, and noticed almost everything sported the club's recognizable emblem emblazoned somewhere. The aviator wings gave William the impression of strength, longevity and mystery. The SAAC block letters inside the wings' borders, and the club's red and black colors were almost as distinctive in the golf world as the green and yellow of Augusta.

The tournament would be held on the Century Course, the same tract as other championships, but the members also had the option of playing another eighteen holes, a rolling and demanding layout called the Gold Course.

"You go off tee number one at 1:30 p.m.," the assistant professional said, regarding the practice round.

"Do you know who I'll be playing with?"

"David Atkins. He's from Tyler, but plays for the University of North Carolina—good player."

"Has he checked in?"

"Yes, I believe he's on the range."

Each station at the practice facility had new balls stacked in a pyramid-like shape, and William found a place to begin. But even before he struck his first shot signs of doubt surfaced; it annoyed and distracted him. Somehow he did not sense he belonged here, not as a person, but as a player; he felt an absence of talent and that his dream had become more fantasy than anything else.

That's the deal with sports—every competitor is judged on performance rather than their position in life. It is the way it should be, William thought, but he quickly realized he needed to address the gymnastics currently taking place inside his heart and mind.

He wondered why he did not choose to be confident, courageous and determined, especially after working so hard to get here, and attempted to settle himself by focusing on the things he could control—starting with his pre-shot routine and the tempo of each swing. Ease and balance he reminded himself, as he struck a variety of shots. The emotional upheaval tired him slightly, and it did not require a brain surgeon to know this was not helpful to the cause. Listening and watching the other players hit solid golf shots impressed him to a fault. "Someone made a mistake letting me in the gate," William whispered, sighing and fighting off the notion he had stolen something.

William counterpunched the negatives; he reviewed Maggie's fundamental ideas he had organized on a laminated note card, but things were moving too quickly and despite his efforts, he could not slow them down. Ultimately, he knew he must learn how to escape from such situations.

"A rose is a rose is a rose," she had said.

"What exactly does that mean?" he asked.

"You are where you are."

He began to wonder if the elements in his approach – the attention to detail, the checking and double-checking, the yearning for excellence and perfection, the almost obsessive belief in discipline and commitment–that served him so well in the law now worked against him in the game of golf; this was a sport that tended to punish a player for over-thinking and over-trying, two concepts William had not mastered.

On the opposite side of the note card, William had mounted a *Peanuts* cartoon he had clipped from the newspaper–one where the characters of Charlie Brown and Linus were at the beach. Charlie Brown had just tossed a stone he had found in the sand back into the ocean. Regardless of how many times he read the frames, they never failed to deliver a smile and sense of perspective; the short-short story also reminded him of an ideal he misplaced all too often–the game was supposed to be fun, especially for the amateur. This was not a life and death situation–presently, however, it felt more important than that.

"Nice going," Linus said. "It took that stone four thousand years to get to shore, and now you've thrown it back."

"Everything I do makes me feel guilty," Charlie Brown said.

The Century Course was designed by pioneer golf architect Paul Sullivan and sat on the site that for many years belonged to the San Antonio Gun Club, a place where cowgirl Calamity Jane once gave shooting and riding lessons, and some exhibitions.

The architect created a unique course amidst tall pines, oaks, pecans, and freshwater lakes and streams, a place designed to use natural resources rather than deplete them. The Century combined old and new, and the holes traveled the same route as they did when originally built in 1919. The course remained one of the most sacred in America, featuring wide fairways that shifted in contour and terrain, thick Bermuda rough, complex greens, and holes that demanded position, management, and solid ball striking as well as length. A natural tributary called Yale Creek meandered throughout, touching more than a dozen of the holes.

Later that afternoon William found his way to the first tee, an elevated piece of earth that looked down on the setting below. It was hot and clear. Something more than history and tradition set the place off by itself; it had beauty and dignity, and like a poet, its own voice.

William checked his yardage book and decided to hit his drive toward the three pecan trees on the left side of the fairway; he would then try to lay up to about eighty yards before hitting his third shot over Yale Creek onto the large green. Playing the par fives backward was something his grandfather taught him as a boy. Patience and a good start are essential, he thought–pars are fine. Historically, the cut line after the second round hovered around the 150 mark, and William figured he would need to utilize every ounce of his talent in order to play all four rounds of the event. His initial strategy had three parts: thinking well, executing each shot aggressively, and a conservative tactic of hitting as many fairways and greens as possible.

"Hello, my name is William Bradford," he said to the young man.

"David Atkins," the youngster said, his eyes not quite meeting William's squarely.

The pair carried their bags during the practice round, focusing more on where to put the ball off the tee and hitting shots to places on the greens where the pins might be located during the tournament rounds rather than concentrating on scoring. They hit extra pitches and putts, took time to test the sand out of the bunkers, and in general watched how the greens responded to certain shots as they moved effortlessly around the course. There was not much conversation between the two of them—some talk about the course layout, a particular technique, tournaments played, that sort of thing, but they did get to know one another slightly. It was late afternoon when they finished.

William was favorably impressed by the young Texan. Turns out he had an excellent game and transferred to North Carolina in the past year from the University of Arizona. David Atkins was less than six feet tall and best described as on the stocky and muscular side; he had a fresh face and bright, timid eyes. Only recently had William become aware that nearly everyone looked younger to him, something he found amusing. He wished he could accept his golf swing as easily and wondered why time and experience lashed out at his certainties rather than strengthening them. Sooner or later, the game exposed a player's weakness; it mirrored life in that way.

During the practice round, William studied the boy's technique and how effectively he put the ball in places that made the next shot easier. Maggie had told him she could write two books about hips, backswings and impact areas, but she believed teaching—real teaching—achieved two things: first, pinpointing the root cause of a problem and attending to it properly frequently fixed minor ones; and secondly, it was the teacher's responsibility to adjust and communicate with the student, not vice versa. She also emphasized it was imperative to make the best score possible on each hole.

David Atkins was a shy boy—young and inexperienced—but William liked that he had so much of life in front of him; he hoped his dreams, whatever they were came true. The youngster had tournament experience and was eager; William also liked that they shared a passion for the game, spoke the same language and for a brief time, chased the same goal. Around dusk they said their goodbyes, and wished one another well in tomorrow's opening round.

"What time do you go off tomorrow?" William asked.

"In the afternoon, around two. What about you?"

"Early. Are you going to the dinner tonight?"

"No. My dad's driving in from Tyler and besides, I did not bring anything to wear."

"If I don't see you, good luck."

"Thanks. You too."

As the young man walked away William noticed the heels of his shoes were uneven and worn. It was an old and odd habit ever since a friend of his and Jane Parker's in San Francisco told them she drew her first impression of a man by the condition of his shoes. She told them not having them polished was, of course, a dead giveaway, but a more accurate barometer were the heels. She told them they were subtle indicators of his station in life, even his soul. The memory had surfaced involuntarily as William watched the boy toss his clubs into the bed of his red pickup and pull away.

8

William arrived around eight for the traditional player's dinner. The function was held in the original clubhouse, restored to perfection right down to the library, lockers, formal dining room and stables; it was a place the city had grown around years before, and located about a quarter mile west of the main clubhouse complex. The invitation-only event was a formal affair and those attending dressed accordingly; it gave players, their guests, and the members a chance to mingle with one another.

The heritage of the San Antonio Athletic Club dated back to pre-Civil War years when Texas was primarily an agrarian state, and the power brokers were large and successful landowners. Through the years enough of the land had been retained to found and build the now famous golf club; a place that in the beginning and for more than three decades allowed only men as members. This, the original homestead, was restored and maintained after the classic-looking main clubhouse was constructed in the mid-1930s. It had enormous grounds, front and back, well-kept shrubs and gardens, shaded with huge pecans, poplars, maples, pines, dogwoods, and flowering magnolia trees. On the north side, there were producing apricot and apple orchards.

"After all," one of the older members told William that evening, "why else did the Scots name it golf?"

"I don't know? Why?" William asked.

"Gentlemen Only Ladies Forbidden," the man said.

"I'd buy tickets to watch Maggie tie into that old rascal," William said to himself, politely moving away.

When William arrived that evening, cars were already parked up and down both sides of the street and a half a dozen or more clogged the main drive as the crew of valets attempted to please everyone. William parked his own car and as he walked across the thick carpet of grass he noticed the new and shiny vehicles–Porches, BMWs, Alphas, Mercedes, Cadillacs, Town Cars, SUVs, convertibles, fancy Jeeps—and figured they would reflect the people he would meet inside. As he neared the house, he could see through the big windows. It reminded him of nights when he and Jane Parker walked past the row houses in San Francisco, and from the sidewalk looked into rooms of the homes that had not drawn their curtains for the evening. They tried to guess who lived there and made up stories about them; hand in hand—looking, imagining, talking and laughing with one another; time passing. He sensed he was more alive then, and he remembered he enjoyed the anticipation of seeing her each day, of missing her, and of needing her; of feeling lucky.

"Sometimes I wonder if life is simply about chance—if it is not any more complicated than that," Maggie said to William one day.

William did not weather the storm clouds of disagreement with Jane Parker in San Francisco, but he knew he had acted badly—not rude or anything, but in a manner that was selfish and self absorbed. He traveled solo now, but loneliness did not crowd him—he was simply alone. In the back of his mind, though, he wondered why he had refused to allow his heart to jump over the wall and take a chance; it was a thought he could not quite outrun.

That night he saw waiters, professional men and women, dressed in white jackets and black trousers serving; the tables covered with white linen cloths and had napkins folded in fan-shapes, with ceramic ring holders around them. He watched people in pairs being poured whiskey, talking, gesturing, moving about, and peering into the many rooms and into one another's faces. He noticed a beautiful young woman and watched her from the shadows as a constant trail of men, young and old, were drawn to her. He noticed how skillfully she evaded their true intentions.

That night, too, he surrendered to the joys of the elite, and their charm. He did not feel all that comfortable, not because he was seated with strangers, or that their worlds were either unfamiliar or intimidating, but because it brought home the fact that many of the walls in society still remained too high for most to climb. It made him think he was not as comfortable in his own skin as he would like to be. He continued to believe Maggie's questions about convictions had some specific purpose, and maybe he ought to be expanding the list with some of his own; then again, maybe her whole point was for him to never quite be satisfied.

He left the dinner about midway through the program and wandered outside; at first to be alone and sniff the air, then back toward his car and his room in the main clubhouse. The staff: golf professionals, tournament officials, social and sales people, ground crews, locker room attendants, and caddies were still at work making last-minute checks and arrangements. He went into the men's locker room and saw more photographs–this time of past champions who had won the amateur championships the five times it had been held here. Outside he walked past an area where the caddies huddled. They were joking and making predictions, drawing lots and placing bets with one another on the eventual winner.

"Suppose to rain tomorrow," a man said, the voice emerging from the darkness.

"Oh really?" William's eyes turned in the direction of the stranger.

Tank Cotton stood about five-feet-eight-inches tall and had an oval face with wide, almond eyes. His neck and shoulders were heavily muscled; his hands and fingers reflections of many years of hard work. He had a baritone voice and his hair was white. The man who stepped forward had a quiet dignity, anyone could see that.

"Yeah, quite a change from today–they said it is going to be nasty, at least for awhile."

"What's your name?" William asked, extending his hand.
"Bradford's mine, William Bradford."

"Tank Cotton. You need someone to work for you tomorrow? No one knows this place better than me or my caddies."

"No. I've decided to carry my own bag–thanks though. How come you guys are still here this time of night?"

"A few of us are just chewing the fat–that's all. Well, if you change your mind, I should be here pretty early tomorrow morning."

"I appreciate it."

"Good luck. Don't forget now, pars are good out there–you don't want to shoot yourself out of it on the first day."

"I'll take eighteen of them. What do you think will make the cut?"

"At this place, with these greens–I believe about eight over–150 ought to get you to the weekend," Tank Cotton said. "Just don't get discouraged–you get the least bit impatient, and you can make some big numbers. I've seen it happen many times."

"I'll take that to heart," William said, walking away. "Goodnight."

"Goodnight."

William had renewed hope from an unexpected source about the first round of competition tomorrow. The uncomfortable stuff from the afternoon had temporarily subsided.

****

2 June
To Maggie O'Connor
Room 212
SAAC
San Antonio, Texas

It has been a year to the day since I received your letter responding to my question about the second ball, and less than a year since our first meeting, where you set the tone and pace after listening to my intentions. So here I am–right where I hope to be; the question is: What now?

I miss not having the option of your earth-bound guidance, but I promise to play each shot without distraction. In this note, however, I want to say whatever comes to mind, whether it is clear, inaccessible or completely abstract. Is that mindless or mindful—there is a difference as you would say.

Today on the practice tee, I had a hiccup—doubt, anxiety, nerves, and a crisis of confidence rose to the surface—but I am calm now. Maybe it is the whiskey or that I've begun to settle into my surroundings. Now that I am here and will strike the first ball in competition tomorrow, I'm wondering what to think. Is it to do my best; make the cut or finish in the top ten? Actually, that particular progression of thought is all wrong—thinking of the results is not what you taught me. Relax, trust in the things I can control, remain positive, and fail better on each swing, right? Yeah—that's more like it.

I must believe that the concentrated, sustained practice has paid dividends and that I am as prepared as any amateur in my situation can be. Man, I'd like to break past some mental barricades tomorrow, but I know there are surprises waiting for me; I hope to embrace them. I hope also—that I understand this event ought to be fun and that it will make me a better player, regardless of what happens. Right now though, I'm applying added pressure on myself. I'm thinking pressure might be a legitimate part of the equation, stress not so much.

You may endorse my nerves as a normal response, but I do not believe you would embrace my goal of simply making the cut. As you said, a player must get winning in his heart and I just cannot claim that truth right now. That's both flawed and honest; there are more shadows than sunshine, more thistle than meadow. Am I somehow lacking in courage? What is wrong with me—am I hardwired improperly? Do I fear failure or worse, success? Why the self destructive attitude? Do I enjoy practice more than competition? Again, this should be fun—the time I've put in ought to be my currency into the event; instead I'm being overtaken by expectation and perfection—self imposed, of course.

I know that my time and effort this last year has been genuine—it has. But I also recognize my efforts will not help cure AIDS or Cancer, or even benefit a child. I have not sacrificed for others, but I have sacrificed a year of my life in order to pursue another selfish, self absorbed endeavor. It is only a game—a beautiful game—but I wonder, and I wander. Can one try too hard and care too much—I ask again, how is that possible, especially if one is willing to put forth the effort? I am a moth drawn to flame.

I have been thinking of Jane Parker lately, sometimes at the strangest moments. Of all the women I've known, there remains a different type of connection with her. If we are lucky, I think most of us have experienced that at least once in our lifetime. It was that way from the first time I met her—that face and those eyes; her demeanor and style, I liked her. Something drew us toward one another, and she was willing to go forward together while I for some inexplicable reason was not.

She lives in New York, but I have no idea if she has married or is seeing anyone. Time passes quickly and I am gradually learning to appreciate that fact. Tonight at the players' dinner I felt alone for the first time. I watched from a distance as men approached a beautiful young woman, and I thought about the good fortune of love, of having someone to share things. I'm an odd duck anyway—here I am on the verge of an adventure and I am distracted by something else. Something is still missing.

Jane Parker believed in writing, that literature enhanced life. Among other things, she taught me that it was important to read and be a learner. Perhaps I have ignored or bypassed some opportunities—like the love of a good woman. Not your minor faux pas, huh?

I know there is more to life than what I am doing right now, but for some reason I am consumed by this golf notion. Do I believe playing well will somehow validate my existence or stamp me with a seal of approval? In our sessions, you stressed the importance of the soul, of playing from there—I think I know as a man, a person, and a citizen that is where validation indeed resides.

Perhaps the absence of single mindedness tonight is a result of all that has occurred during the last few months. Maybe I'm just feeling blue or black or dark, like I am destined for the shadows; invisible in a way. When I decided to take a hiatus from the law and move back to Texas, golf offered a challenging distraction, but now life has gotten in the way again. I question my approach to life about as often as I do my approach shots, both significant factors don't you think? I believe if you read my words written tonight–well you'd think I've gone mad. I sense that I am going to get waxed tomorrow. My brain is lost, my heart more so.

William set his pen down and switched on the radio. The San Antonio Missions and El Paso Diablos were playing a minor league baseball game. It is just a game, he thought. Soon he was fast asleep.

9

Thunder and lightning greeted William early Thursday morning, the first day of the tournament. It was still dark outside when the alarm broke the silence and he pulled the room curtains apart. Rain peppered the window. This was no cotton shower, he thought, thinking of the West Texas farmers he had heard discuss the weather and how they never complained about rain under any circumstances. Tank Cotton had mentioned a weather change, but this type of severity was the last thing he expected or wanted. At daybreak, what looked like sheets of rain pushed by the wind danced across the grounds like ghosts, and William wondered if it were possible for moisture to fall any harder from the sky. He stood at the window in his pajamas, drinking his third cup of coffee. Going off at 8:22 a.m. meant arriving at the course by seven. He did not like to rush his warm up. Now, his mind worked on some alternate plans.

He decided to go to the course anyway and found the starting times delayed as he expected. People milled around, talked quietly over coffee and breakfast, or sat by themselves. William read, reviewed his personal notes, and went over his yardage book. He scribbled down some ideas to pass the time: drive it in play, be prepared to scramble, twenty-eight putts and patience. He also wrote the name Jane Parker several times in the margin, like a love-sick kid does on the cover of his school notebook.

A couple of hours later the rain stopped and play began. William had seen Tank Cotton earlier that morning and the man asked him again if he wanted a good hand on his bag. William hesitated, but made what might have been the most critical decision of the day–to carry his own clubs and turn the veteran caddie away. William liked toting his bag; he grew up that way and embraced its tradition and solitude; besides he felt more athletic. But the possibility of rain and wet conditions began to concern William, especially when it applied to the rules and pace of play. He wondered how he would deal with rain gear, umbrellas and towels, and keeping his hands and the grips of his clubs dry. His inexperience showed and some anxiety set in; at the last second he tried to find Tank Cotton, to no avail.

"Mr. William Bradford of Star, Texas, on the tee," the starting official said.

"Don't lose this thing on the first day," William repeated as he bent down to place his wooden peg in the ground. "Pars are good."

He wished his fellow competitors luck and showed them what ball he planned to play and how it was marked. He checked his pocket for his yardage book, but when he reached into where Maggie's bracelet was supposed to be, it was missing. In the confusion, he had left it on his bedside table.

When it was his time to play, William stood behind the ball to visualize the shot at hand and went through the pre-shot routine he had practiced thousands of times during the past year. He knew the first shot and a good start were important. As he prepared to swing a few rain drops struck the bill of his cap and the thud-like sound distracted him. "Back off, back away," he told himself. "Do not dare hit this thing before you are ready."

He ignored the warning and made a quick, short backswing that produced a shot that curved left and landed in the thick, wet Bermuda rough. There was a difference in being unlucky and being reckless, he thought, walking to his ball; of thinking well and reacting poorly.

The Sullivan-designed starting hole at the San Antonio Athletic Club presented the player with some choices in regard to strategy and shot selection, but was not considered one of the most difficult on the course. The fact it was a straightforward and fairly short par five with a wide fairway provided hope. "It gives the player a chance to warm up a bit," the architect had said when the course opened for play in 1919.

The hole ran directly away from the tee for about 290 yards, turning downhill for another 150 before heading back uphill to a large, elevated green some 510 yards away. Yale Creek, the narrow winding ribbon of white water that ran throughout the course crossed the fairway roughly sixty yards from the green. A solid drive to the top of the hill granted the possibility of going for the green in two shots and an eagle or birdie opportunity. The alternative, of laying the second shot to a distance just short of the creek, also gave the player a chance for par or better.

William consulted his pin sheet for today's flag location; it was positioned only five yards from the back edge of the large, hour-glass-shaped green. A long, deep sand bunker protected the front of the green and a smaller one lay on the other side; a shot struck long was destined for thick rough where bogey became more likely than not. Other than the putt, the second shot was critical to playing the starting hole well.

William realized patience and composure were important aspects of golf–anything really. Let the game come to you, he thought. In the practice round, he had experimented with both plays (going for the green in two or taking the less risky route), and found it required one of his best drives in order to take a chance. Hooking the ball into the rough left him but one choice–to place his second stroke as close as possible to the hundred-yard mark; to "pee-wee up" as the old timers back in Star called it. He hit his third shot into the middle of the green, maybe twenty feet from the hole. He sighed when he saw it land safely; he had maneuvered successfully out of trouble and figured to be able to make a par five at worst.

Overhead, the clouds and passing storm had reversed course. There was no thunder and lightning so play continued and the intermittent showers predicted now looked almost certain, but not a single forecast predicted what arrived that morning. A slight sprinkle had begun on the walk from the fairway to the green, and William popped open his umbrella. He marked his ball, repaired the divot, and lined up his putt. It was not a difficult putt, a slight left-to-right breaker, but also not one the percentages favored the player making. Two putts and move on, he thought. As William addressed the ball the heavens opened and a hard, cold rain pelted down, and the wind gusted. Was he prepared to be unlucky? He backed away, but by the time he struck the first putt, his clothes were drenched, his opened umbrella set to one side tumbled end over end through the back sand bunker, and his mind was not far behind. By the time he missed the second putt of less than four feet, things had suddenly changed.

"Play on," the tournament official said, as the group walked toward the second hole.

William gathered himself: There are some things–a bad pairing and certainly weather conditions in which the player has no control–that must be dealt with effectively on an emotional level. Slow down, he thought, knowing today's elements, if they held for any length of time, would be a challenge he needed to somehow welcome.

William stood beneath his umbrella on the teeing area of the second hole eyeing the contour, his course notes from the day before, and his heart. The fact he gave a stroke away on the previous hole bothered him; he had wanted to start well, but he knew nothing could be done now except to concentrate on the task at hand. The rain, whipped by the wind, moved sideways.

"Stay in the present," he told himself.

The short par four turned slightly to the right. Yale Creek ran the length of the hole, also on the right until it curved left, and protected the front of a two-tiered green. Hardwoods and pines lined each side of a fairway that narrowed and slanted toward the water. Although a driver struck perfectly would leave a short iron to the green, William considered it too risky and chose to hit a four wood; his target the forked tree in the left center of the fairway. He made a quality swing and put the ball right where he wanted–in the fairway, about on hundred and fifty yards from the hole. He consulted his pin sheet; the flag was on the lower level, ten paces from the front edge of the green and no more than fifteen paces from the water.

"Aggressive execution, conservative strategy," he said aloud, as he addressed his ball. "A six iron ought to be enough to get home."

William hit another solid shot straight at the flagstick. "Be right," he said, watching it sail in the air. But it landed a couple of feet too far, ending up on the second tier of the green. Now, rather than a possible birdie opportunity he faced an unusually fast downhill putt; getting down in two strokes would be a good effort under any circumstance. He nudged the ball and watched it gain momentum and race six feet past the cup. He rimmed out the comeback putt and now stood at plus two for the day; two greens in regulation and six putts. Fail better, he thought.

William knew he could not be distracted by his mounting score; rather he must center his complete attention on each shot ahead. If he had the courage and discipline to stay on that path he could live with whatever number kicked out and was posted on the scoreboard at the end of the day. He did not want to accept less.

Golf is an unforgiving game. Sometimes the difference between prosperity and disaster is miniscule and this reality can crumple the best of players on occasion. William was no exception as he attempted to find the right combination of resilience and acceptance to counter his poor start. Somehow or another, he had to believe in himself. This past year he had raised his expectations as a result of Maggie's instruction, by winning the qualifying event and with practice; he was more seasoned and knowledgeable, but the fact remained this was the first time he had competed at this level. These things and a steady rain followed him to the third tee.

If possible, the rain and wind came even harder as William made par on number three, a short par four. The score stabilized him momentarily, and he sensed a slight surge of optimism and confidence. Golf is a fickle game, but he realized the responsibility to play well rested with him, and him alone.

Number four was the second par five on the front side, an S-shaped hole of about five hundred and thirty yards and not long, even for a medium hitter like William. From the beginning he figured the hole presented an opportunity to be aggressive, and that was his mindset when the driver cracked from a solid hit and the ball landed perfectly, again in the left center of the fairway. William hit four wood to the knee of the second dogleg on his next shot and was left with a straightforward seventy-five yard approach to the green. He felt confident as he addressed the ball and took dead aim at the pin located in the back left portion of the green. But he tugged the shot slightly sending it just off target, to the left.

"Hang on," he said, watching and bending his body to the ball's flight.

Although he could not see the shot land from his position in the fairway, William thought the ball probably ended up in the left-hand bunker. He hoped it did not bury in the wet sand, but figured he could get it out safely onto the green, make par or bogey and move on. As he neared the putting-green area he did not see his ball.

"Do you see my ball?" he asked, thinking it may have cleared the hazard and run down the hill into the rough behind the green.

"Here it is," one of his fellow competitors said.

Suddenly, he spotted it, too—pin high, but stuck beneath the back lip of the bunker in a nasty and impossible looking position. It looked more like a half-buried shell on the beach during low tide than something he was supposed to hit.

Maggie had stressed knowing the rules of the game on each of his visits to Fairway Farms. She emphasized golf consisted of more than merely hitting shots and understanding the rules often gave the player options and the opportunity to make the best choice possible.

William decided to play the ball as it lay and in doing so, struck it three times before dislodging it from the original position. A short pitch and three putts followed before the number ten appeared on his scorecard. There was silence from his fellow competitors, and William felt the shame and embarrassment connected to the situation.

Now standing at seven over par after four holes and almost on the cut line Tank Cotton had projected a day earlier, there was no one to consult except his own heart. He had smashed head-on into one of the game's challenges and wondered if he could muster the level headedness to bounce back; or possessed the determination to rebound from such a broken effort and come back stronger. The questions required answers.

Following the round and several whiskies, William opened the rule book he had left in his room alongside Maggie's bracelet. Not knowing the rule or having the composure to ask a tournament official for advice had cost him as many as five shots on one hole, possibly more in the long term. It was clear he should have opted to drop the ball as near as possible to the spot where the original ball was last played. This was basic stuff and a serious breach of responsibility on his part.

During the remainder of the round, William's inexperience surfaced further as he failed to put his previous mistakes behind him as he was taught. Instead, he allowed one missed shot and one terrible decision to turn his training upside down. By hitting a middle iron into the water on a short par three and then attempting an improbable one to begin the back nine, he had become a player who had abandoned his preparation.

The wind and rain continued. However, the eventual outcome rested more with his behavior than the weather. Things had gone badly and there was little relief, even less to praise. Maggie had told him he would miss shots and golden opportunities, but few rounds of golf go according to plan. She told him it is not what happens, but how the player responds to what happens that separates competitors. It is the interesting part of our spirit, she had told him.

"What a joke," he said aloud, as he trudged up the eighteenth fairway.

Suddenly, nothing in life made sense, and he was drained of energy. He had struggled in the pursuit of excellence the entire year, and discovered on a summer day that success does not come easily nor is it guaranteed by hard work. William signed his scorecard for a total of eighty-five strokes, the highest in the field. At best, he was disappointed and relieved this part of the day was over. Seeing an old college friend in the distance momentarily lightened his emotions.

"I think that went well," William said, greeting his friend.

"How do you stand?" Guy McKenzie asked.

"Dead last."
"How did you do that?"

"I made a ten-foot putt on the last hole."

William let his old friend buy him a drink at one of the pubs in the main clubhouse. Guy McKenzie ran the family business in San Antonio and lived in an older, exclusive neighborhood near downtown. He was a member at the San Antonio Athletic Club.

"Why don't I call Caroline and we can have dinner down on the river," Guy McKenzie said. "There's a place there that has great food and makes fresh guacamole at your table."

"No thanks. I'm afraid I would be poor company tonight. Next go around, okay?"

"I understand. Hey, whatever happened to that writer friend you were seeing in San Francisco? Are you guys still together?"

"We lost touch awhile ago. I believe she's working in New York."

"What was her name?"

"Jane. Jane Parker."

"That's right. Pretty woman. I liked her."

"Yeah, me too."

Back in his room and a bit dazed, William sat down and replayed every shot. He wondered what he learned today, and calculated the best score he might have shot, if he had kept his wits and executed properly. He wondered why this type of train wreck had occurred at this particular time; after all, he was halfway intelligent, somewhat of an athlete–the answer had to be out there somewhere.

He poured himself a whiskey; the drink burned as it went down and before long he was back at it. He figured he would need to shoot sixty-five tomorrow to have any sort of chance to make the cut, something he had never done. He was strangely optimistic.

****

To Maggie O'Connor
3 June
Room 212
SAAC

Well, I think that went well today, don't you Maggie? Let me get this out of the way from the start–I forgot your bracelet and my rule book and the fact that I left both items behind may tell you everything you need to know.

I feel badly for playing the way I did–that goes without saying. I must confess that I have questioned what I was thinking; actually believing I could compete with all these fine players after such a long layoff from the game. Still, even if I never competed in another round, there is no way I would not take the game seriously. Blessing and a curse, right?

What bothers me the most (other than the embarrassment of my score) is that I messed up on the mental and emotional fronts today. Granted, my execution was poor, but failing to know a fundamental rule was an absolute deal breaker–there is no excuse; I accept full responsibility. Today was not a dress rehearsal and I simply blew it. You are where you are, right?

By the end of the round today my eyes had filled–that's a laugher, huh? A forty-five year old man–Texan, lawyer, bachelor, golf athlete, fictional winning in the heart type of player completely ambushed, and I responded like a kid that had lost his first Little League game. The concerning part is that I lacked courage, resolve, composure, patience, skill, confidence and balance; almost everything you taught me I did the exact opposite. I failed, failed again, but time after time I did not fail better. In this way, I shortchanged the game and myself.

Honestly, I feel a bit defeated. I know that it is the wrong take on things and that you would scold me for whining, but I have never quite felt this degree of disappointment in myself. I suspect all hearts get crushed occasionally. Perhaps that was the basic point of your question regarding my beliefs and convictions, right? There are definite chinks in my armor and I am not proud of that, but I am willing to fix them.

I remember my grandfather told me about his time overseas during World War II–he did not talk about it much, but he did say to stay alive you had to work at it; to die you simply had to quit.

(Later):

I feel better this morning–raring to go. I figure I've wallowed in enough self pity for a lifetime, and to be honest, it is out of character for me. Intellectually, I understand what occurred, and what things require corrective action, but I know too that the application is the difficult part. Today there is opportunity for some redemption.

I honestly do not believe I have a sixty-five in me although that is the score that would bring me in at the 150 mark. You would perhaps nudge me away from that type of thinking and towards doing my best on every shot–I believe you would think that the deeper victory. My best, however, has become a mystery overnight and a far cry from when I arrived in San Antonio on Wednesday.

One thing the experience has illustrated–golf is not simple. It tests many skills physically (timing, coordination, balance, and technique), but perhaps the ultimate test is in the emotional and mental parts: overcoming fear with resolve and certainty, maintaining poise when adversity strikes, remaining relaxed and staying in the moment, without distraction. I wonder: How does a player remain confident when he or she is not playing well–is it faith, optimism or conviction? The weather forecast for today is sunny and clear; my heart is too. It's just a game, right?

****

The sun was just breaking the horizon when William headed toward the practice range to prepare for his second round. He had always enjoyed this time of the day, when all things were waking. Due to the weather yesterday, tee times were adjusted and his group was scheduled to go off first this morning. As he walked past the eighteenth green he watched a groundskeeper meticulously do his job, and noticed heavy dew on the ground and fog lifting off the lake nearby. The pines stood tall and straight. As he passed the scoreboard, he saw that even par was leading the tournament, and that his practice partner, David Atkins, had withdrawn. Later, he found out the young man was playing poorly and following the eleventh hole, walked off the course.

"What would make him do such a thing?" William asked.

"Don't know," the official said.

It soured his stomach to hear such a story, and William knew the incident would trail and torment the boy for years to come; and if he was not careful, it would become easier to repeat the episode the next time around. He remembered the worn heels of the young man's shoes, how they needed repair, and wondered if he had somehow become the family's meal ticket. It was not an ideal way to begin the day; he felt badly for the boy.

The practice session went well: He hit wedges, short irons, longer irons and some shots with all his woods before moving onto the short-game area, then the putting green. He was calm and decided to concentrate on the tempo of his swing rather than mechanics; to enjoy the round, but play the game. More than anything, he wanted to be grateful for what he had.

On the first hole, William hit a short drive and again had to lay his ball up behind Yale Creek. He then hit his third shot fat off the wet turf and dunked it into the water, eventually making double bogey. Not the start he imagined as he walked toward the teeing ground of the second hole.

William finished birdie-par-birdie for a score of eighty-two. He signed his scorecard and turned it in before cleaning out his locker and heading home to Star. He ran into the tournament director and apologized for his poor play, but the man was generous with his comments. As he drove slowly away, he took one last look around; his eyes filled, but he accepted complete responsibility for his play.

****

To Maggie O'Connor
4 June
SAAC Parking Lot

I can hardly claim to be the victim when good people die too young, when others work three jobs to support their families, and so many more important things are going on in the world. That said my performance in the competition stings.

I know it is not the appropriate moment to address these issues, but I'd like to get something down on paper and out of my gut. I really do not even know what I am writing–is that not crazy? Stream of consciousness, I guess; a fresh stream.

Why do I play? Do expectations match my ability? Are expectations even good to have? Do I have technical flaws in my swing or are the main barriers in my heart and mind? Are there concrete answers to the questions posed? Is my criticism constructive and necessary or over the top? What must be resolved first? If I address and repair the main issue(s), will the minor ones automatically be corrected or improved?

What did I learn today? What did I learn yesterday? Did I try and fail, fail better, and do I know what those terms mean? Maybe I thought I was ready for this level of competition after winning the qualifying in Abilene, but perhaps that was more luck than skill. Should my response be to work harder, take some time away to gather myself or is finding perspective in my own way part of the deal? There is finality in the moment.

William turned right out the parking lot and headed west toward Fairway Farms. There was the letter to read; he had intentionally left it at her place to read following the competition. Obviously, he wished it were under different circumstances.

Mesquites and mesquite scrub, huisache, prickly pear, and yucca gradually began to mix with the oaks as he got closer to Calahan and Fairway Farms. He made his way through the small towns and across rivers; a train snaked its way through the countryside, sometimes running parallel to the highway, and wildflowers, waist deep and colorful, stretched along the edges of the road for miles. As dusk neared he noticed a caravan of sheep gathering in the fenced corner of a pasture while cattle and horses grazed elsewhere. Windmill blades twirled slowly in the hot wind, and San Antonio faded in his rear view mirror.

It was dark when William arrived at Fairway Farms; the stars and a thin crescent moon made for a beautiful evening. He went upstairs, retrieved the letter from Maggie's desk, and took it down to the lower garden where he pulled open the seal. The moonlight became his lamp.

In her note, Maggie said she had once seen a play in New York (*Camino Real*) by Tennessee Williams where many of the characters contended with the idea of growing old and becoming irrelevant in the process. She wrote in one particular scene Lord Byron gave an unforgettable speech that made such an indention upon her she made sure she wrote down the lines when she returned to her hotel later that evening.

For my good friend William on his return:

"Lately I've been listening to hired musicians behind a row of artificial palm trees instead of the single pure instrument of my heart. For what is the heart, but an instrument that turns chaos into order, noise into music. Make voyages, attempt them. There is nothing else."

Book Three

"I'm a fatalist," he said. "I consider I am rejected in principle. My work is and, through my work, I am. If it's accepted, it's miraculous or the result of some misunderstanding."

Arthur Miller
American Playwright

"There is certain pathos to education. It deprives us of our certainties."

John Updike
American Writer

"There is one choice possible, and the test of whether one has chosen rightly can never be made by considering what is best, only by whether one has rightly judged what made one happy…"

Isak Dineson
Letters from Africa

"Just live your life so that you would not be ashamed to sell the family parrot to the town gossip."

Will Rogers
American Humorist

"Reading maketh the full man. Some books are to be tasted, others to be swallowed, and some few to be chewed and digested."

Sir Francis Bacon
Of Studies

1

William returned to Star. There he hoped to regroup, clear his heart and mind of the debris that had built up, and begin again. The question was: How did he plan to go about rejuvenating himself to the point he was satisfied with the outcome?

He had been a typical Texas kid. Not a whole lot of money growing up and by some standards, not much even now; it had never been a principle motivation. Going to the circus, a rodeo or on vacation to Galveston Island or Corpus Christi for a week each summer was a big deal. So were playing Little League baseball, swimming with friends at the city pool, or going out for a cheeseburger and frosted root beer on a Friday night. Summers were always fun, just not long enough. He wondered how one reclaims the joy sealed into those days.

He wanted to smile again without settling for less; he wanted to find the courage to love and let go, whatever the situation. There are moments now when he looked into the mirror and saw the face of his grandfather, but the reflection disappeared quickly. There are memories of his grandfather, though; of taking coffee with him on the screened porch of the old home place outside Star, and then later on Jefferson Street. The pair would rise early and the old man would pour his grandson some milk with a little coffee added. The old man drank his black, out of a saucer.

William did not embrace all the things in the small town where he had returned; he looked around, listened to certain conversations and recognized he had changed.

Mostly, William had more questions than answers, but he wondered if the world could be understood by any single human being. He had been reminded again that trying and falling short are part of the journey, that attached to the human condition is the basic ideal of attempting something and failing to hit the mark; he also had come to believe there is something good in sustaining such an effort without being guaranteed anything. He still thought he would learn the most about golf through dedicated and precise practice; that it was a process without a finish line, one filled with ups and downs which ultimately must be enjoyed and endured. He figured the same principle applied to living.

"None of us are immune from self deception," Maggie said: "And in the end, few will know who we really are."

****

To Maggie O'Connor
1 July
Star, Texas

Dear Maggie,

I have not put all the pieces of the puzzle you have given to me together. You are such a straight shooter and I know there is help buried in the messages, but right now I cannot muster the clarity to understand what you are exactly saying to me. I think sometimes a person can want something so badly they lose perspective going after it, no matter how noble or honorable; a person can be too close to the situation and often not see what is before their very eyes.

I realize I need to laugh and locate that perspective, but I've been home for about three weeks now and find myself at a place I am unfamiliar—rock bottom.

The harder I work and press forward, the more pressure I apply to my efforts and the worse I become. I'm considering taking a break from the game for awhile despite having nearly two months of summer left. I admit being surprised by how much of my heart and soul I've put into these past months and by how deeply the outcome, especially the disappointment of my performance at the amateur championship affected me. It's strange, because for so many years my life has sailed along so smoothly; the view from where I sit now is quite different.

I ask: Does the process require getting worse before getting better? Why are bad habits so hard to dismiss and like a dandelion, so easily resurrected? Why don't good habits work that way—why do they require longer taking shape? Can you have limited self confidence and consistent doubt even though some ability is present? What is courage—is it grace under pressure as I have heard, being resolute in the face of fear or something more? I wonder if I would flourish if placed in an environment where other players approached the game as I do – instead of feeling odd and foolish as I sometimes do for caring too much and wanting to do my best. Where is my athletic compass—I seem to have misplaced it somewhere? Did it ever exist? What does it look like? Is it me rather than its needle which does not know the way? Perhaps I am the needle.

Frankly, I am humbled by the experience before me and more aware of the journey of others. Yesterday, I drove by a local strip mall–like I have on numerous occasions–and wondered for the first time about the people working there. Everyone has their stories.

Knowing that you thrive on playing around in the vast real estate of the heart and mind, I imagine you would ask me to answer at least the following (as you have):

Why are you playing golf?

Is it fun?

What are your beliefs and convictions?

What are your goals, visions and intentions?

What is your behavior?

You'd warned me to be wary of what I hoped for; you also pointed out that win or lose, I'd be the same person at the end of the day. Maybe that is the deal. Maybe…

As for golf, the truth is I am neither a confident player nor do I have a winning attitude inside of my heart. I wonder–am I missing the will to win? I have patience and perseverance, but suddenly I am concerned about my competitive flame and if I possess (like you suggested is required) the diligence of a laborer. Throw in a little shame to boot and there you have it. Perhaps I figured it would be easier; I wonder what you would say about that.

I remember you once told me about a painter-friend of yours and how she believed that someone who took pleasure from their work would have less difficulty dealing with poverty. What about poverty of the spirit? I know–you believe work cures everything. I wonder what happens if I decide not step up to the plate–if that decision will haunt me? Two words follow me now and I am obsessed with them: Jane Parker. I had an opportunity at love and I not only failed to embrace it, I bypassed it altogether. I wonder if my actions illustrated more selfishness than courage; more self absorption than giving–less of everything that eventually counts? Maybe I ought to find the trust and faith necessary in letting go–if so, that may demand addressing parts of my past. What is this place called rock bottom anyway?

****

The summer unwound toward the fall. William continued to work on his game, but his results did not match the effort. In September he was spent, and relieved to put his clubs away for awhile. He continued to write in his journal and pen some letters; this time he sent one to an old friend.

5 September
Star, Texas

Ms. Jane Parker
305 West 89th Street
Number PH
New York, NY 10024

Dear Jane:

I decided to send this note to the last address I had for you. With some luck I hope it finds its way into your mailbox. I think it has been nearly five years since we've spoken to one another and I apologize up front if this is an intrusion in any way.

Jane, I am traveling to New York in early October and if you are not busy and can spare some time for dinner, lunch or just coffee–you name it–I'd like to visit with you while I am there. There are some specific things I want to do, but my plans are open to fit your schedule.

You have been on my mind for some time and I'd like to catch up with your life. I will certainly understand if you decline. How is your writing? Are you still working for the magazine? Written that novel? Are you doing something completely unexpected?

I left San Francisco last year and returned to Star, Texas to start not necessarily a new life but a different one. Remember my grandfather—of course you do—you guys hit it off pretty good when he paid us a visit out West. Well, he has passed on and I now live in his house—it is a wonderful place, full of memories and goodwill, and it has always been a safe haven for me. There are just some places like that, I suppose. I put the law on the back burner, and am unsure how long it will remain there. Actually, I'm unclear about a lot of things right now. In the meantime, I renewed my friendship with golf, and found it to be a humbling experience.

Among other things, I'd like to see The American Museum of Natural History, Saint John the Devine, and Central Park while in New York. I'll be glad to explain why.

I hope we can meet and say hello to one another again. No obligation of course.

Best regards,
William

Parker
305 West 89th Street
Number PH
New York, NY 10024

20 September
New York

Dear William:

You can imagine my surprise when your note arrived last week. It has taken me a few days to gather my thoughts and decide if meeting you would be a good idea.

As you know, I left San Francisco due to our breakup and could not get far enough away. Our footprints and memories were too prevalent. For awhile I was ambivalent, but decided I had to save myself by doing what was right for me and New York was about as different as anything I could imagine. I had loved you with all of my being and was forced to face the truth–it is amazing what a person can do in that situation. The hurt continued for awhile, but I have steadily reconstructed my life here.

New York has been a positive place for me and of course, barely resembles the West Coast, certainly San Francisco. For one thing it is a much larger. The mindset is different too: The chatter of the street may be alienating to some, but I have found New Yorkers sentimental; helpful but guarded. There is so much talent here–from the musicians playing in the metro to the painters, actors, playwrights and others–all coming here with a dream on their sleeve and the will to do whatever is required to make it. There is something honorable and noble in that idea, that ideal, at least I think so. The city has a definite edge to it; sometimes I walk for hours and never fail to be surprised. The characters come in all colors, the beauty in various shapes and forms, and the architecture cast its shadows onto the earth and sea; somehow the inconvenience is worth it. Nothing is perfect, right?

I left the magazine last year to write everyday—freelancing to make ends meet and writing fiction on my own dime. It is a risk. I've learned that novels require time, inquiring thought, patience, faith, and a sustained effort; not much different than anything else accomplishment requires. It also demands honesty—otherwise the words will not ring true; line by line as they say. It is a tough road, but I am not complaining I have chosen words and ideas as my racket, something my parents never quite considered a real profession.

Of course, I do not fly every day—there is a certain momentum to it all, but I have some moments. One must prepare to be lucky in New York—I had heard that before, but really did not know what it meant before living here, of being a resident in one of the many neighborhoods. You have to be ready for it. I try to stay in the present with my dreams and not get too far ahead of myself, but I believe I am prepared to be lucky and I have faith that I will make my way if I keep my focus and do the work. No doubt, I am out there on a limb, but I like the freedom of being responsible for the choices I have made. Writing and reading are important to me.

William, I'd like to see you—there are some things to say. Please call when you arrive and we will arrange a time.

Always,
Jane Parker

****

On a Thursday evening in October they met for dinner at a French bistro on Amsterdam Avenue near her home in Manhattan. The night was cool and fresh, like following a good rain. He had arrived first at the cozy, inconspicuous restaurant on the Upper West Side and was seated near the front window when he saw her enter the door. She was a beautiful creature, at that moment perhaps more than ever before. He stood as she approached the table.

"How are you?" he asked, as she took her seat.

"Fine," she said, placing the napkin in her lap. "I hope this place is okay."

"Perfect."

It did not take the pair long to break the ice; they had started as good friends and despite the pain created by their past love, found a certain comfort in one another's company and conversation. They were strangers now and each felt the mystery and tension that fact delivered, but as the evening wore on they concentrated on staying with the selective good times of the past as well as touching upon the lives each were living now.

William told her, in greater detail, about leaving the law and returning to Star. He told her about his strange obsession with golf and of meeting Maggie O'Connor. He told her of Fairway Farms, the gardens and the letters, about what he knew of the relationship between Maggie and his grandfather, and the reasons he had traveled to New York. He told her of his dismal performance at the state amateur championship and how his preparation had melted away into something completely different than he expected or was prepared to encounter. He told her how the experience affected him; how his reaction to it surprised him and made him wonder how something so insignificant in the scheme of things had monopolized his life the last months. He told her his despair had nothing to do with playing badly (although that bothered him, too), but more about what he considered to be the absence of character and courage. He told her he had failed to display either when called upon to do so, and that he had lost his way. He told her he was strengthened by her presence.

Jane Parker listened; she had always been a good listener because she believed listening reserved time for a measured response. That night she dressed in all black. Her face, with its high cheekbones and tanned complexion, blended perfectly with her dark brown eyes and golden-brown hair; her eyes were clear and sharp, bright. It was an expressive face, a gorgeous face. She had a playful smile that accompanied her modesty and grace, and there was an innocence that had stayed with her. Her body remained lean and athletic; William had always liked the way she walked and the style in which she dressed. Although her energies were now centered on words and ideas, Jane Parker knew about the things William discussed with her–in San Francisco they had played golf on several occasions and watched many sporting events together. She was a knowledgeable fan.

"Sorry," he said. "I'm going on and on about this. It's bordering on the ridiculous."

"It's okay. It's sort of interesting to see you this way."

"What way?"

"Oh, a bit unnerved."

"Hmm?"

"Wine, Monsieur?" the waitress asked.

The French accent came from a small woman. She was dressed in jeans, a white shirt with a black necktie, and a white apron that tied at the waist. She had dark eyes and eyebrows, and short hair, dyed blonde.

William looked toward Jane Parker.

"A bottle of the Medoc, please," she said, pointing to her selection on the menu.

Later, Jane Parker told him certain essentials are demanded of the writer as she suspected, of most things. She told him that above all else the story matters most to her, but form and style, narrative, point of view and, of course, the characters mattered, too. She told him good fiction had an almost invisible unity, and writing it was tricky business; and for her, challenging, painstaking work. She told him writers had to write the story in which they believed and write it honestly, but the reader also had to be pulled into the journey and care about the characters; become part of their conflict and resolution. Fiction has an opportunity to get at the truth without preaching, she told him.

She told him she believed the writing was either good or not. She told him again she had come to believe time and inquiring thought were the real keys; that only writing was writing, and she knew of no other manner in which to advance the imagination than by going to her writing table every day. She told him every writer knows rejection and among other things, battles fiercely against the dullness and a wandering mind.

"I try to work at the same time each day," she said. "It's the best way I've found to do work in a concentrated fashion and provoke my best effort. Still, there isn't anything I've ever done that I didn't want to do better."

"Do you ever question what you are doing?" he asked.

She told him she believed a writer had to be committed to the work, because the odds of success are great, and like a prize fighter, they are solitary animals. She told him writing was also a process, one where there were ups and downs, frustrations and disappointments galore, but enduring them and understanding them was the only manner in which writers earned their way. Patience was everything, she told him.

"Have you ever written a perfect sentence?" he asked.

"Now that's a whole other issue—sort of like your second ball question. Is there such a thing as perfection?

"The answer is no," she said, "but I've read some things that are as close to perfect as I can imagine. Truman Capote was a great sentence writer."

She told him it was easy to despair about not writing eloquently, of constantly having agents and publishers turn away one's work, and of inching so slowly toward excellence.

"Have you published any of your fiction?" he asked.

"Not yet."

"How do you keep going?"

"To be honest, I'm not certain I will ever write anything as masterful or powerful as the things I've been reading lately, but as long as I have a chance, how can I stop."

"You're right, I know you're right," William said. "It's just that for my entire life I've put myself in the position to move forward, but at the last instant I flinch, self destruct, produce funky swings and thoughts or simply back away. Right on the brink, then boom–turn in another direction or something. It is as if I leave everything on the practice range. All that work toward a certain goal and when the chance to accomplish it or put my best foot forward are within reach–I react as if I no longer care. All the sweat, then I sabotage the effort. What is that all about? How does one break past that line some cross easily and others do not attempt or care to pass at all? I wonder about that. I wonder what I believe and why my actions often contradict those beliefs. Does that make sense?"

"Look, William, to me writing is more about hard work than anything else. Like I said, each new project is like beginning all over again, regardless of how well the previous one was written. Each day is different, too. What's important is to realize it's generally later than we think, and that balance and passion are crucial parts of life; every time out counts.

"Maggie was right to tell you to be bold and adventurous–to make the voyages," she said. "I've never known you to–well–to whine like this."

"I know, it's pathetic," he said, laughing at himself. "I don't like it much."

That night, William and Jane Parker talked primarily about golf and writing, and how the two subjects intersected with one another. They discussed politics and the state of things affecting the world. They danced around asking anything too personal, but the curiosity was there, similar to the way a person's sense of humor often disguises the pain. Early on in the evening he noticed Jane Parker was not wearing a wedding band, and outside of the bistro, at the last moment, he blurted out the question he could not hold in any longer.

"Are you married or seeing anyone?"

"I'm going to be out of pocket tomorrow, but I'll be in East Hampton on Saturday. Would you like to come out? We can spend the day at the beach."

"Sure. What time?"

"There's an early train out of Penn Station that leaves around seven. Do you know what the un-popped popcorn kernels at the bottom of the sack are called?"

"No."

"Old maids," she said, grinning as she turned and walked away.

William watched until Jane Parker disappeared around the corner. His heart pounded and he smiled, easily remembering every detail of the evening.

William woke early Friday. He took his time, something he had not done in awhile. He had coffee, breakfast, and read the newspaper before leaving his hotel and setting out through the neighborhoods of the Upper West Side. Along the way he passed Lincoln Center and Julliard, cafes, bookstores, shops and stores of every size and nature imaginable, and scores of people. An hour or so later, he found himself standing across the street from where Jane Parker lived. It was a simple, well-kept row house of maybe three stories, with a stoop. An entrance to Riverside Park and a view of the Hudson River were at the western end of her block. He wanted to see her, to tell her some things he held back last night, but decided to wait. She cared about him for so long—wouldn't she want to know? The thought sounded arrogant and desperate; tomorrow would be soon enough.

William crossed Broadway, Amsterdam and Columbus avenues before arriving at the American Museum of Natural History, on Central Park West. There he climbed the marble steps that led past the statue of a mounted Theodore Roosevelt toward the main entrance of the museum. Once inside, he paid the suggested admission price and asked and received directions from the guard at the information desk to the place Maggie had described to him. On his way, William learned Theodore Roosevelt read a book a day, wrote thousands of letters, received the Nobel Peace Prize, was considered the pioneer of the conservation movement, and assumed many other roles in his American life, besides serving as the nation's president and vice-president. On his way, William passed dioramas of North American Mammals and ocean life, and gazed at a majestic, ninety-four foot blue whale suspended from the ceiling in a place named Milstein Hall. Off an adjacent corridor he found the Hall of Biodiversity, where an exhibit explored the South American country of Bolivia and delivered him light years away from the place he stood a few days earlier.

In a small corner of the North American Forest section of the museum, William found the exhibit he had traveled to see. It was smaller than he imagined, a three-dimensional miniature of an Iowa farm behind four panels of Plexiglas, one for each season of the year. The white farmhouse sat back from the highway, as did its red silo and barn nearby; the setting–complete with rolling hills and fields against a painted background–reflected the charging force of nature's calendar. Within each section was the wildflower garden Maggie spoke of; her words rang inside his head as his eyes followed along to the things occurring (to plant and animal life) above and below the surface of the earth.

"It's not the alterations on the surface, but the activity beneath it," she had said. "The forces of nature are never idle; there is constant movement by all members of its cast."

William had never doubted her words or ideas regarding patience, trust, and maintaining attention on the process; what had begun to have legs, even brief moments of clarity, were the things that actually contribute the most to our performance in life.

Later, he boarded the number seven bus that took him north on Amsterdam Avenue. He took a seat by the window where he watched the cityscape pass frame by frame; he took in, among other things, small, tended gardens on vacant lots, kids playing ball on asphalt playgrounds, ethnic eating places and neighborhoods, shoe shops, fish markets, sidewalk vendors, and buildings with fire escapes climbing their outside walls and wooden water towers on the rooftops. An old woman rang the bell and got off with her grocery cart at 110th Street. William exited the back door and walked up the street to the place called the Cathedral Church of Saint John the Divine.

There he made his way through the sanctuary; past the stone carvers and the various alcoves of memorials–to the victims of the genocide in Armenia and the Holocaust in Europe, AIDS sufferers around the world, New York City firefighters, and various poets and writers. His eyes searched the beauty of the stained glass, the sheer enormity of the place, and the ancient tapestries that hung from the walls. He listened as a children's choir rehearsed, their voices pure and clear.

He had come to the gothic church to see the biblical herb garden in the back. He opened the wooden gate and went in, finding a seat on a stone bench beneath an olive tree. Except for two peacocks, the garden was empty.

****

To Maggie O'Connor
October
The garden at St. John the Devine
New York

The day is cool and clear, a classic autumn afternoon here in the herb garden of the Cathedral at St. John the Devine. What a treasure in the midst of chaos. The church, without exaggeration, is magnificent and larger than anything I've seen; it speaks for itself. But the place where I am now is every bit the great structure's equal. Of course, ultimately the place is a sum of its parts.

The garden is protected by a simple wooden fence, waist-high with a small gate. The herbs are planted in square plots and have name plates in Latin and English. There are several olive trees that have smooth black bark, and skeleton-like limbs that take on a deformed look as they reach in all directions. I like the benches made of stone and wood; they are simply built. Two peacocks are wondering around the garden and except for their occasional echoing scream of "help, help" my presence does not seem to disturb them as they peck the ground, and look about; they appear to be right at home, confident in their brilliant and colorful feather coats. I like it here.

St. John is an Episcopal Church; it has a full-time soup kitchen that feeds people three times a day, vespers on Sunday evening, and later this month anyone can bring their animals to receive a spiritual blessing. I am told even the circus animals come. What a sight that would be to see an elephant in line with a house cat. I read too that during the Christmas holidays there is a hundred-foot evergreen decorated with white doves; they are origami doves, folded to perfection, one by one. There is some sort of school on the grounds, just beyond the gates. I see young boys and girls wearing uniforms; they are laughing and their faces look so young. This is a calm place; it celebrates life.

Earlier today, I visited the Museum of Natural History and found the wildflower garden you told me about, the one you compared to our own secret garden. Again, I was surprised at its size compared to the herd of African elephants, the planetarium, the sequoias and whales, and dinosaurs. Nature–TR had a keen eye in nurturing and protecting it. Like this garden though, size does not matter when one thinks of impact.

It is the personal take on things that matters anyway–I believe that. Find out what makes an indention on the soul–that's the deal, right? I was surprised that the backdrop for the flower garden was the farm in Iowa with its red barn, silo, and simple headquarters. It was interesting to see how the plants and animals react to the seasons, whether it is snow covering the ground or the first crocuses in spring; whether it is November or May–things are always going on.

Less is more sometimes.

It is growing dark and the grounds are closing. A crooked line of men, women and children stand beside some steps outside the church's kitchen waiting for their evening meal. It is hard to take my eyes off them. I'm heading to the Hungarian café and pastry shop nearby to devour some fresh bread, lentil soup, and a few pages of the book Jane Parker loaned me. It is about a small town in Ohio, its characters linked together in each story. From what I gather, the stories challenge the fantasy-like purity of small towns; they too are blessed with human folly and imperfection. It's strange–I have felt these things since coming home. I like my grandfather's place, but something is missing–different. Is it the attitude toward others people consider important, or something else? I think it is difficult to figure this stuff out. I wonder if I am in the right place.

Tomorrow, I travel by train to East Hampton to meet Jane Parker. I hope it is as good of a day as this one has been. Something has awakened inside of me, and I'm slightly more alive.

****

Jane Parker picked William up at the train station in East Hampton and drove him to the Hunting Inn where she kept a room; sometimes, especially during the winter months, she wrote there, but walked the beach year around. She was fond of the local joints and the characters who frequented them in the off season, yet it was the sea and solitude that drew her to this place. The ocean was less than a mile away; there she felt the breeze on her face and absorbed the power of the waves crashing inward. There, too, she watched the tides, the sailors, and the fishermen come and go, and the stars sprinkling the night sky. There was no pretense here, not in the places she had become fond of visiting.

It had taken some time, but she regained her own peace and power here amidst the weeded dunes, the foam and the swells, the shells tossed onto the white sand, the wet sand. In the summers, she sometimes fell asleep and briefly did not know where she was when she awoke. She liked putting on sweat pants and a long-sleeve shirt on a summer evening when the sun started down and everything began to cool. She read here and thought here. She discovered and recovered here. The tides erased some things, and the salt had helped to heal her heart.

"Right on time—did you have any trouble?" she asked.

"No, your directions were perfect."

"I like the train, especially this time of day."

"It was great."

William got into the car and they drove to the inn, where they parked and climbed aboard two bicycles. Jane Parker handed William a backpack and told him that was his only responsibility of the day.

"What's in it?" he asked.

"Lunch."

They rode for a few blocks on the village's main street, passing a movie house, the storefront of the local newspaper, a butcher shop, and some beautiful homes before turning right on Beach Road, where they rode in single file at a steady pace toward the unknown. William had no idea what to expect. In a few minutes the road curved slightly and began to parallel the dunes. They stopped, slid their bikes into the rack, and made their way on foot to the white beach that ran along the Atlantic Ocean. Again, the day was almost perfect and the sun glistened off the water as wave after wave pounded the earth.

"Wow," he said.

"It's beautiful, huh?"

"Unbelievable."

"Let's walk for awhile."

They did, almost in complete silence. There were a few others on the beach: couples, families, a few dogs, a man with a kite. It was a place that easily absorbed all comers and granted them everything they needed. Jane Parker was indeed at home here. He could tell that by the way she dressed; by the way she confidently moved and knew her way; by the freshness of her face; by the clarity he observed in her heart and mind. She was a beautiful woman, he thought once again, stealing a glance and admiring her as often as possible. It was a warm day considering, somewhere in the sixties, and she took her sweater off and wrapped it around her waist. They talked, but not about anything serious. He wanted to say something to her about the way he felt, but lacked the courage of the previous morning when he stood alone in front of her building. He waited.

Later, they sat down for lunch. The day was passing quickly, and he did not know what it held. It was a quiet section of the beach, slightly back from the water. They spread a blanket and sat on it as the sun darted in and out of the few clouds. Thunderheads looked to be building in the distance and the ocean breeze played in the beach flora. They finished their sandwiches and lay down side by side. The sun warmed their faces and the sleep rested their minds.

"I'd like to tell you something," William said, slowly waking.

Jane Parker was already sitting up and looking out at the sea. "I didn't want to wake you."

William told her he had been selfish in so many ways, pursuing a career and interests he figured could be better achieved alone, without answering to anyone. He told her he had come to realize that instead of representing courage, it did not; instead of leading to a fulfilled life, it led to an empty one; and rather than giving, he was always taking. He told her he understood most tigers do not change their stripes and he probably could not become a jaguar in a day, but in some cases the past is not indicative of the future. He told her he had reached the conclusion that love and balance are key to life, and love matters most of all. He told her he hoped he was not too late, that his running away had never made him free, only a prisoner of his own ineptitude.

"I know that I caused you so much grief, and that you loved me for almost a decade without much of a return on things. I don't know where you stand or how you feel about this, but I can honestly say I love you, Jane Parker, and would like to somehow know you better."

"Isn't it odd," she said. "Just when you let go of something you've longed to have for as long as you can remember, it comes your way. That's sort of ironic don't you think?"

She told him she planned to leave for London the following week to be with someone else, a man she has been seeing for awhile and who has asked her to marry him. She told William if things go as expected, she will move to Europe permanently, probably around the first of the year. She told him the man was a journalist, a man of honor–a good man who truly loved her. She told him she loved the man, too. William listened as she described how they met by chance at a book reading in London, how they later shared dinner at an Indian takeaway, and afterward had dessert and tea at a place called Louie's.

"Along with writing, that is my life now," she said.

"What's his name?"

"Jack Madison."

At the train station, they embraced and he kissed her politely. She held his hand for what seemed like eternity and told him she was glad he had come.

"Me, too. Tell Jack Madison he's a lucky man."

"All the best, William," she said, watching him board the train back to the city.

"You, too," he said, waving to her before he disappeared into the elongated carriage.

He took a seat by the window and watched as she walked, then drove away. The hurt was real and strange—she deserves the best, he thought as he leaned his head against the pane. The moon had disappeared behind the clouds and a hard rain began to hit against the glass. He closed his eyes.

On his final day in New York, William wanted to make a couple of stops before catching his plane back to Texas in the early evening. Again, he rose early, but felt surprisingly rested. Several whiskies the night before had helped.

Sunday morning in every city is the quietest part of the week. Central Park was no different as he entered the giant piece of rock and green from the south, moving past empty ball fields, a timeless carousel where music played and children boarded hand-carved wooden horses, a boat house and fountain where a jazz trio was setting up shop, and a pond where people sailed remote-control boats, and some brown ducks swam in rank file, while others sunned themselves, unaffected by the crowds. There were runners, bike racers, skaters and skateboarders, couples—some reading the New York Times—and others allowing the sun to shine on their faces.

Jane Parker had told him the space saved New Yorkers and he believed it as he continued north, past statues, the Metropolitan Museum and a place called the Great Lawn, a large oval of green where balls, Frisbees and kites flew in the air, dogs walked their owners, people sat with their coffee, and a replica of the Globe Theater stood, its outdoor seats empty. William exited the west side of the park. He wanted to take one last look at Jane Parker's place before heading back to the hotel to pack, check out, and head home.

William continued to the end of her block that dead-ended into Riverside Park. There he found the flower garden Jane Parker had told him about, the one maintained by the people who lived in the neighborhood. He took a seat on a bench that provided a good view of the garden and the Hudson River beyond. He watched as several sailboats glided about aimlessly on the water, and a couple of tugboats helped a freighter move out to sea. A young woman, perhaps in her twenties, with long legs and black hair, was there, too. She seemed shy, a bit nervous and ill at ease as she pulled on her cigarette.

"It's a good view," she said, breaking the silence.

"Yes, yes it is," William said, surprised. "You come here often."

"All the time. No matter what–it's a place that helps me remain grateful for what I have, without begging for more."

"Happiness and perspective are good things to have in life."

"Yeah. You can pretty much forget about the rest."

On his return to Texas William penned a letter to Jane Parker thanking her for her time, and again extending his wish for all the luck in the world regarding her new adventure. He attempted to be brief, yet wanted to make every word count. In his journal, he was harder on himself, especially for behaving badly and allowing such a beautiful and loving woman to escape into the shadows of his memory. Jane Parker was gone. I shall be the worse without her, he thought.

****

To Maggie O'Connor
25 October
Star, Texas

Dear Maggie,

You remember the woman that I spoke to you about on occasion—Jane Parker? Well, I have just seen her for probably the last time in my life, and it strikes me how I have allowed someone who loved me (and turns out I loved her) to slip away into the night. After years apart, she has found someone else—what do you expect, right? My heart is bruised from the news.

I am home again and despite the jolt, less lost than before the trip. As always, I wonder why I have sacrificed love and balance for my own selfish endeavors or searched for answers at the expense of gratitude. When I returned to Texas from California, I thought this amateur thing was a noble goal; it was challenging, provoked my interest, and required passion and hard work. But perhaps my energies were targeted upon all the wrong things. I am learning life is not always a game. Perhaps the hardest truth of all is that I may have a heart a few sizes too small.

I think that I've finally begun to comprehend what you've been trying to teach me—that validation comes from within ourselves and not from some external source; the outside simply overtakes us sometimes. The more I realize that fact, the better I am able to understand that one must have the courage to face the truth squarely, and to reveal themselves–to let go of what we cannot control and fail if we must. That is important in the process of learning, don't you think? I believe will is part of talent, and I might even argue it is a more crucial than all the unapplied potential in the world.

I am not sure how life unfolds and teaches us–if it is age, experience, luck or some other combination of factors, but there had been a time when the future glowed with promise and the sky was not the limit; somehow I was certain it would turn out that way. Now, I look back and wonder what that feels like, if it is true or just some foggy, delusional notion. Was it a mistake of destiny? Time passes, but I am still the optimist; the attitude is just different, that's all. My hope is that the resignation I've moved toward these last months will lift and the optimism returns.

The package he received in the mail delivery from Jane Parker was neatly wrapped. Inside he found a letter which he set aside and a beautifully handmade book based on the designs of the biblical herb garden at Saint John the Devine. The book was maybe fifteen pages, and included a diagram of the garden's layout and what herbs were planted where; sort of a bird's eye view of the small plot of land that lay quietly behind the colossal church in the northwest section of Manhattan. Each page contained an original watercolor of an herb–sage, rosemary, thyme, angelica, flax and dill, among others–along with its official name and an explanation of why it belonged in the garden. On the last page was a description of the text and type of paper along with Jane Parker's signature. The binding of the book resembled the colors of the peacocks he had seen roaming the grounds.

****

Parker
305 West 89th Street
Number PH
New York, NY 10024

31 October
New York

Dear William:

Thank you for writing and letting me know you were visiting New York–it was good to see you again and travel back in time. I thought it might be painful, but it was not, it was good–at least for me. We started as good friends and I believe that is how it will always be. Maggie was right about having only one set of memories, and you are forever part of mine. I will never flinch from that fact.

The present takes me to London to be with another man and for a long time I could not even fathom that possibility. William–he is a good man, a truthful man, and he cares for me deeply. He has taught me many things.

I wish you well in Texas or elsewhere, and hope you find everything you are searching for. You have always been a bit of a wanderer. I have enclosed this book and it speaks for itself. My only regret is that I did not attempt to paint the olive tree. It is filled with such strength, character, grace, and beauty; and belongs in the garden.

I remember we spoke about Maggie's questions and more than anything, I am pleased that we saw the moon on Saturday afternoon from the beach. To me the idea of even looking for it during the day, when indeed its existence is most in doubt, speaks of hope and faith, and an optimism that is the best humanity has to offer. Too often, we do not think to even look up. Simple pleasures, huh? The moon smiled at us that day. Did you know there will be a blue moon next month?

I hope that you do not give up on golf quite yet–I believe you have some unfinished business to attend to. And for Pete's sake please do not abandon the law or love–you have so much to offer. I see it, do you?

There are some similarities between golf and writing, but I am not sure I am qualified to make the connection. I do believe any author must write for themselves and write the story they want to tell; I do believe the story leads the writer and that the writer must allow the character(s) to tell the story; I do believe there will be ambivalent and muttering times, but that one must find the will to keep going; I do believe that even with a sustained effort each day, of trying to put something on paper, nothing may come; then again it may produce a germ for a novel, a short story or something unexpected. We advance through a process of doing, similar to the secret garden Maggie referred to so often. The first story I finished allowed me to write the next one–that's all.

Be well, and I hope luck is your playing partner.

Always,
Jane Parker

****

William thumbed the book again, pausing to read the introduction:

"One summer between semesters at university I helped my family move to California. It was a good summer, one where I discovered a love of writing, water colors and the sea. That summer too, my mother and I planted an herb garden in our backyard.

"I did not think of herbs again until I moved to New York and found them in the most surprising of locations. The herbs and this garden will always remind me of that summer and of time passing."

Book Four

"I am sick and tired of being sick and tired."

Fannie Lou Hamer
Civil Rights Activist

"Throw your hat into the ring."

Theodore Roosevelt
From the book *Hatless Jack*

One service more we dare to ask –
Pray for us, heroes, pray,
That when Fate lays on us our task
We do not shame the day.

Rudyard Kipling
Writer/Poet

Well I've got a hammer
And I've got a bell
And I've got a song to sing
All over this land

The Hammer Song
Words and music by Lee Hayes and Pete Seeger

To Maggie O'Connor
New Year's Day
Library on Jefferson Street
Star, Texas

Telegram: The Hunt for Perspective

I have taken some time to gather my thoughts since returning from New York. You were right the City is an interesting place, and I was taken aback by its subtle beauty, inspiration, and pace. I was surprised too by the feelings stirred by an old friend—my best friend really—Jane Parker. For some reason, I cannot quite let her go.

The two of us picked up where we left off several years ago. Timing is everything I suspect; for those that seek to push the envelope of possibility or for those who choose differently. It is part of the human condition to try and to fail; part of its greatness. On that first evening I realized that I loved Jane Parker—something only a fool would discover so late in the game, especially when the evidence was in the clear for such a long time. Now I know my misplaced adventures hurt her, and it is something I deeply regret. Screwing up things at the state amateur last year pale in comparison to the significant whiffs I made where Jane Parker was concerned.

What was I thinking all these years? It is like you said—perhaps when we don't know what to do or where we are going, we have begun our real journey. If so, I now begin in earnest. Retracing my steps for a moment, I must ask: Do I know what love is?

The short answer is yes, I think I do. For all the confusion love brings, it's simple really—one either loves someone or not. I admit that it is possible for our memories and emotions to play tricks on us regarding matters of the heart, especially in a time of loss, but this is not so in this particular case.

Jane Parker is with another man now, and all I can do is wish her the very best in life. She deserves it. From a strictly unsentimental viewpoint I wonder what I expected, since I treated her like an afterthought for the most part of forever. I guess I figured true love lasts; that ultimately whatever I did, however selfishly I acted or however long she had to wait–she would. How crippled is that train of thought? Do you believe there is one true love in a person's life? It does not necessarily have to be the first person, but one true love–do you?

Looking at things now, I believe I've acted a bit delusional. The perception of being a man best suited for a single harness does not ring true today, yet it is a perspective I might have to accept. There is no question I have recognized for some time the absence of calm inside of me. Perhaps that is one of the reasons I returned to my home base of Texas; maybe it is partly responsible for propelling me towards this golf madness. From the beginning, you told me that even if I attained my golf goal, I'd still be the same person. Maybe that is why you stressed playing the game with the heart and soul, because the idea was only partly about golf; just as the second ball question boiled down to the first ball. Am I right?

One could argue I'm deliberate to a fault, and that I am unable to get out of my own way in almost everything I do. However one slices it, I realize I am the fundamental issue, that's the truth of the matter; I wonder if I have the smarts to figure out how to get further along, in a good way. I miss our sessions; they nudged me back on track.

Maybe I'm simply an obsessive, compulsive person that is eager to please; if so, that sounds like an awfully short leash to be on. Regardless of how I wish to express it, the effort has gotten me to the point of looking to my heart for some answers, and the idea has delivered humility, and the hope for unarmed truth and unconditional love to my doorstep.

Among other things, time and place have shoved life (and golf) into a better perspective. That said I once again plan to pursue the goals we originally discussed, with a renewed vigor and purpose. Life goes on as it must and I am obliged to keep moving, treating golf as the game it is and the law as the profession I may wish to practice once again.

I will go to Fairway Farms later this month and when I return, begin training for the state amateur qualifying in April. It is again in Abilene. To give it a final go is the right thing to do and my plan is to work hard, attempt to correct some technical and emotional flaws, and when I practice and play, do so with a concentrated mind. Jane Parker told me there was a certain momentum to writing, and that the only way she had advanced her imagination was by going to her writing desk each day and diligently turning her words into sentences, paragraphs, pages, chapters and finally, a manuscript. She told me she figured her work depended upon what happened in her study that day; that every word counted, and that the writer must pay attention. I figure that applies to golf, too.

Before I begin there are three conditions I am determined to meet: to do my best on every shot, to enjoy the process, and to play and practice confidently, with a will and fearlessness that will not back away from winning or coming up short. If I am fortunate to make the tournament again, I do not wish to be satisfied with just being there; nervousness and intimidation are separate things. There is also a balancing act where the past is concerned, especially in golf. I must learn from my mistakes in order to prepare more thoroughly and not repeat them, but know the past has nothing to do with the present task at hand. In tournament golf, distraction of any kind is a negative thing and the player must center their focus upon what to do right rather than what went wrong.

So my structure is to formulate a game plan (within the confines of my everyday life), and systematically go about achieving it. For some people, that approach would prove boring, idealistic or simply foolish, but Jane Parker told me she writes for herself and she writes the stories she wants to write. She told me that writers often chart their progress in different ways, but the common objective is to do the work. She told me Hemingway counted words; that he worked in the mornings standing up in oversized slippers, with a number two pencil. She told me if he planned to go fishing the next day, he would write extra the day before, because he viewed writing as a debt of honor, a debt he figured had to be paid. She told me she believed a writer had to read in order to write and that in doing so must ask questions along the way. But what questions? Ultimately, she believed time and inquiring thought were the keys.

I'm not blessed with the kind of clarity she spoke of–I have too many keys on my ring and I'm certain some no longer open any door. Besides, I'm a drifting amateur and Jane Parker is an advancing professional. I believe now that even the elite athlete can over think and over try. Sometimes I feel silly spending so much of my energy on a game. Time is fleeting. But I believe in dreams–always have, and despite every reason not to be, I am an optimist.

Golf draws me in and I am fortunate to have the passion and joy in playing. That is a good thing and there is no need for further apologies. Work is a good thing–love and balance are good things. Some recent images stick in my head as I keep moving – the boy and his dog sitting side by side at the beach looking out at the ocean; the gulls clowning and flapping in the sun; the olive tree living in the old garden; and the moon and stars hovering, dancing together.

2

William visited Fairway Farms and found things in order. It was supposed to be a day trip and the gardens and trees had taken on the look of winter. It was the time Maggie spoke about—when nature was active despite the evidence. She had compared the situation to the two oceans. Both were beautiful, but the Pacific's beauty was immediate and complete, universal; whereas the Atlantic's beauty took time to comprehend.

Hector and Maria were in good health and, of course, had taken splendid care of the place. They had two more grandchildren since William last spoke with them; the twin girls, Isabelle and Zavalla, were born on the day after Thanksgiving. While there, he also spoke with Elizabeth Nathan on the telephone.

"How's the weather," he asked.

"Beautiful, but then it is good most of the time out here. Plan to come this way anytime soon?"

"Not that I know of—I just got back from New York."

"Oh," she said.

William told Elizabeth Nathan about his trip, and what his plans were for the coming months. They discussed Fairway Farms briefly and wished one another the best. She told him once again he always had a place to stay if he decided to head west.

Later, William found his favorite spot in the lower garden and wondered about the idea of trimming his sails back, of finding the resolve necessary to change course and move his heart toward the right place. He wondered if he made things more difficult than they had to be, if his constant search was more of a blessing or a curse, and if any of the answers he sought would ever work themselves into the clear. There were no guarantees, of course, but he treasured the day when the iron door yielded and the path through the thicket became visible. He figured the best he could do right now with golf was to stay on the path he was traveling.

It was leading him somewhere, elsewhere. "Why do I play the game and what do I want from it?" he asked, aloud. The question required an honest answer.

Suddenly the late afternoon had turned into evening and William found himself sitting in the dark. A galaxy of bright stars and a half moon looked down on him. Maria had told him goodnight an hour before when she brought him a glass of whiskey on a tray. His eyes were riveted upon the shadows at the edges of the moon and his thoughts drifted even further, to memories of his grandfather. The drink relaxed him and he decided to stay the night rather than travel back home to Star.

His grandfather, William Polk Bradford, was born in Houston, the son of Andrew Franklin Bradford, a sometime musician and businessman, and the former Emma Scott Wayland, who had been a chorus line dancer. Shortly after completing his education, he and his young bride, Anna Clara, made their way to West Texas, where he began working as a land man in the oil business. He never left. He had come as a tall and handsome young man with a shock of rich, black hair and a look of determination in his eyes. He was distinguished looking, characterized by his earnest approach to life and by all accounts, spoke directly and simply. Always the gentleman, he had full command of strong language when wanted and enjoyed cigars, poker and bourbon whiskey. William remembered him having a fine sense of humor, that he liked a good story, and laughed easily. Anna Clara died unexpectedly that first year.

William Polk Bradford believed personal independence mattered and never wavered from his beginnings as an intense and unspoiled young man. He believed until his dying days the difference among men boiled down to energy, purpose, willpower and determination. He believed in knowing the facts before spouting off and that respecting others mattered as much as anything. He believed in striving to improve every day, and being open to ideas that did not necessarily agree with his own was important. Above all, he considered working hard the key ingredient to success, regardless of how it was measured.

"There is no shortcut," he said.

In William's mind, he was a man set apart; a man whose home honored family, literature and sport. He was a man of vitality, originality and intellectual boldness. Writing appealed to him, he once told his grandson, but he eventually turned to business, and whether or not he had taken the right course was a lingering question throughout his life.

The game of golf was a fixture in his grandfather's life, too, and for as long as William could remember his clubs were always part of his luggage. In those early years, the old man would take the young boy to his club in Star, and there they would spend time practicing and playing for an endless number of hours. The idea the game was to be played with joy and pleasure, but taken seriously transferred easily to the youngster. William was a blank slate, a sponge that absorbed it all—it was the way in which he was taught. The remarks veered toward the positive, even though the old man knew failure was part of the game.

"You don't have to play golf, you get to play golf," his grandfather said often.

The man taught his grandson to play from the actual hole on the green backward. He taught him to putt, chip and pitch the ball before moving back into the fairway for approach shots, then further back for longer shots. But he was neither a professional teacher or player and later told William he did not believe he possessed that kind of ability even if he had had the time to develop his talent to the fullest extent. It was not the only hitch; the old man did not care to play the game for prize money. He cherished the idea of being an amateur, of striving for excellence for excellence's sake, and considered it the purest form of competition. The old man offered no apologies for his unconventional and idealistic approach to the game, and his voice still resonated in William's heart and mind after all these years. He helped establish in the boy the rules by which he played the game, and the ones, too, by which he valued the game.

So it came to pass that William's approach mirrored the amateur tradition honored by his grandfather. It was a gift passed to him by an older man on summer days from an aluminum teaching stool, his face in the shadow of a worn fedora. William loved those days when they would hit balls and talk about things in a calm way. Everything slowed down. From the beginning, the youngster was taught golf was not simple—it tested coordination and timing, challenged a player's courage and poise, and uncovered weaknesses. William felt lucky to know such a game.

The noise of a barn owl broke William's trance-like state. He paused and sighed deeply, but his mind returned to golf. From the woodland garden nearby he could hear the slight wind move through the pines, and the sounds from the preserve beyond were like a clarion call reserved for a winter night, tweaking the eerie stillness. He tasted the whiskey, closed the sweater collar around his neck, and leaned his shoulders against the back of the chair, returning.

His grandfather taught him about the fundamental techniques of putting, which as with any shot, included grip, address, posture, ball position and the path of the stroke itself; all things needed to create the proper pace. They hit putts from all angles; short putts mostly, but breaking putts, mid-range and long putts, too. These were shots that comprised almost half the strokes during a round and it was important to make them work in a positive way. Be still, nothing moves unnecessarily—not the bill of your cap, not your sternum, and certainly not the breaking of your wrists, he told him. He encouraged William to find his own style and stick with it.

William Polk Bradford knew what he was doing, but he was not a taskmaster with his grandson. They worked at their games, but it was fun and they enjoyed the process of improving. The game required practice if a player wanted to play well and the combination of movements had to work in the proper sequence, with a combination of grace and power. His grandfather displayed a rare quality—a purity of the heart for the game he loved and respected, and for life.

Often the pair played for ice cream cones or root beer floats. The old man would challenge young William to get a short pitch up and down or to hit a low punch shot to escape trouble. They talked, they walked in silence, they saw late afternoons turn to dusk, and on many days, especially during the summer, they were the last to leave the course. His grandfather taught William to be decisive, and to never hit a shot before he was ready.

"You will succeed through determination, timing, imagination, hard work, and discipline, but there must be joy, too," his grandfather said.

3

William returned to Star and the following day began his training and preparation from scratch; a similar approach Maggie had taken with him in their first session together. There were things to resolve before he started to hit balls and practice on a consistent basis. He had less than four months until the qualifying event in mid-April, and William first wanted to determine how to study, train, and learn; how to project himself outwardly from his soul. He smiled, especially when he imagined his soul located somewhere behind his belly button launching his golf ball to some green in the distance—this year in Abilene and Fort Worth. Was it an exercise that would train him for life through golf, or was he finally beginning to build his life in a way that would transcend anything he wanted to do? He knew this: He was a human being who happened to play golf, not a player or lawyer who happened to be a human being. The validation would come from having the courage to live appropriately; what that meant remained up to him.

In her sessions, Maggie asked her student to search the corners of their heart and soul in order to ask questions and find an answer or two; now it was to time to decide how to present himself—what to emphasize and what to withhold.

So he began—at his grandfather's writing table, with his heart on his sleeve and his mind wide open. It would be a new glove, clean clubs, and a stack of balls. It was about solving problems, patience, and knowing the answer lies in wait, if he will ask the right questions and bring forth the diligence his grandfather had mentioned. William went back to Maggie's original questions to find out where he stood, and attempted to come up with at least one hundred others of his own. He decided he knew little of others, life, love or himself. He also decided that being aware of such things was not a bad place to begin.

****

To Maggie O'Connor
31 January
Writing table

Telegram: My Hunt for Conviction

The questions you handed to me when we first met have been a constant thorn in my side, but have spurred me on when I did not think I had the stamina or inclination to do so. I thought maybe you might like to hear a few things I have to say on the subject, since conviction and beliefs may go to the heart of the matter.

How does one arrive at certain beliefs and convictions anyway? Do they grow naturally? What does it take to nurture and encourage them; and why, if ever, do they sprout wings? Everyone has them: the banker, baker, greengrocer, newspaper man, doctor, scientist, iron worker, shopkeeper, nurse, men and women of all stripes, ordinary and extraordinary.

How do we find out more about the rules that govern our lives, the ones we are duty-bound to observe and respect, and the things that we have found to be the leading components in how we conduct ourselves? I do know that it requires commitment and fortitude to abide by them sometimes, especially when they are out of fashion. I do know if we remain learners these ideas may change. I do know that not every matter is completely black and white and that one must be skeptical of such certainty.

After kicking a few tires in my lifetime, my general feeling about these ideas and ideals—of conscience, faith, hope and reason—is that our behavior says a lot more about us than our professed beliefs. I'm wondering: Is it better to give than receive? Can love be a joy when it is unreturned? Do we have a choice in the matter? When you love someone and are no longer with them—are the memories selective and good; always true? Are they real, imagined or some combination?

I recall one of your question asked if I believed in free will or thought my fate predetermined. The question is even more open-ended than mine about the second ball and clearly requires a lot more thought, but recently I read about an eastern philosopher that compared the idea to game of cards. She said, "The hand that is dealt you represents determinism; the manner in which you play the hand represents free will." It illustrates, at least in my view that in many instances there is no finish line where beliefs are concerned, especially if one is open to learning.

My stab at some questions of my own did not deliver many solutions, only a chance to think out loud about everyday life. I hope that is not a shortcoming.

What does it mean to live appropriately? Going through life or in reading a good, really good piece of fiction, how does one know what questions to ask? What does time and inquiring thought mean? What is heart? What is love? Is my image of it comprehensive and respectful, or fragmented and self destructive? What is the soul? What is the over soul? Are we ever as good or as bad as we perceive ourselves to be?

Why is the sky blue? Should anyone be a slave to time? Is golf more science or art? What is process? What is practice? What is the difference between strategic and tactical? Is expectation good? What is courage? Are women braver than men? Is motion action? When we let go and hit a golf shot, why do we feel as if we are not trying our hardest? What is the difference between being alone and being lonely?

What are people for? What is the unconscious mind? What is the zone? Can we consciously tap into it, practice it? Are any thoughts original or do we swipe most of them? How does one locate their life's work? What makes a poet, or a cartoonist? How can the CEO of a national hamburger chain be hired to run a major airline? Why does the idea of perfect or eloquent paralyze us? Is precision and perfection the same? Why do we get up each day feeling differently? Does anyone need to be resigned to anything?

What are politics? Why do bad things sometime happen to good people? What is fair? Do I need to be interested in everything to be curious? Is doubt okay? What is confidence and how is it captured?

Does confidence arrive from a solid performance or does the good performance result from confidence? How is it maintained? Is attitude confidence? What is the difference between an optimist and a pessimist with hope?

Does power corrupt? What is happiness? How does one judge it? Can one become accustomed to happiness if they never have known it? Should satisfaction last? What is calm? Is tolerance a value? Why is it difficult to change course; change habits and change beliefs? Can one learn to dare? Is the desire for excellence and ambition the same thing?

Does one either possess imagination or not? Can one learn grace? Can I ever be as good as my dog thinks I am? What is more powerful—words, pictures or ideas? Does place matter? Why is it some days I plod and some days I soar? Why do I feel, regardless of my hard work that I am a slow learner? Why is clarity elusive? With regard to learning and progress, do we spend the majority of time on the plateau? Why can't I make my body do what I intellectually understand it ought to be doing in the golf swing?

Is it ever permissible to lie? Are truth and honesty the same thing? What is considered a master? Can we master anything? Is idleness okay? Are some rules made to be broken?

Who are my heroes and heroines? What do I base that admiration upon? What is certainty? What is integrity? Is finding out what I am for more vital than knowing what I am against? What is passion and commitment? How does one balance the two? What is greatness? How is success measured? How should one approach life—by being practical and reasonable or by living each moment as if they are prepared to die? Does making choices and being responsible for them have a direct relationship on how our society performs? What is solitude?

Is happiness better judged by height or width? Is a golf swing better judged by length or width?

Does everyone have some form of prejudice? Does diversity make us stronger or weaker? Is racism or other bigotry based in ignorance? Are human beings subject to folly? Is trying enough? What is empathy? Even though a person cannot experience every situation, horror, or tragedy, can their imagination take them there? Do dreams come true? How does one learn to be grateful for what they have? What is required of us to be humane? How would I like to be remembered? Am I my work?

Why do I often feel as if I am sailing into the dark? Why is it that I cannot get out of my own way? How does one learn to hit every ball with their heart? What does it feel like? What is jazz? What is the difference between: I'm a great putter vs. can I really play well without a perfect swing? What do I want to continue to believe? What beliefs do I wish to change? Why do we impose limits upon ourselves? In general when we believe we have a choice—are there more than two? Is there only one right answer?

Do we learn best by trial and error or trial and success? What do I know? Is self-appraisal the same as self absorption?

As you can see the questions come fast and furious; they are far easier to pen than answer. Perhaps it is why time and inquiring thought are the keys. The questions clearly reach beyond my knowledge and experience, but that is their glory, their gift. Maybe, it is by seeking the answers that we stumble onto the germs that lead us onward and upward; where we find the strength to remain curious about our potential and the courage to remain a learner.

4

William reached the qualifying site in Abilene in time to play a practice round prior to the actual event the next morning. Tomorrow would be a year to the day he received the news of Maggie's death. He planned to carry her bracelet with him just in case his athletic compass teetered. He owed her that much–to give it his best shot in her presence. Perhaps more importantly, he owed it to the game, and to himself.

He was not concerned about the outcome nor did he give much thought to his future in tournament golf. He had prepared as best he could and remained faithful to being every ounce the amateur player, devoted to the game, but in a way that did not consume all his interest or talent. Tournament golf demanded a slightly greater effort. However, he figured he had come back to the middle of that equation, where he belonged. At some point in his training he concluded he had digested more than enough information and it was high time to find a way to push forward. Each shot played must be struck with minimum distraction, and things he had no control over–the weather, an annoying playing partner, the pace of play or even the occasional errant shot should have minimal impact upon his performance. It was all about commitment.

As part of his training, William had begun to study writers, painters, poets, dancers, composers, rodeo cowboys and others whose performances resonated from some special place. He discovered a conciseness and clarity in them; an attempt at few wasted lines or words or movements–where everything played a necessary part of the whole. It made sense to him. The artists and the elite athletes had an insistent quality, the courage to put their heart and soul onto paper, canvas, stage, and the earth. Most were compelled by the work, and intent on improvement; all able to muster the faith and endurance required to do so.

He became interested in certain aspects of their biographies: their natural talent of course, but also their will, their reaction to rejection and disappointment, and the crucial moments that led them to become masters in their professions. How did they sustain themselves in the face of challenge and when the odds were stacked against them? How did they fight back and what did they draw upon? Were they aware effort guaranteed nothing?

Jane Parker told him she agreed with Maggie's perspective about perfection, that she, too, viewed the possibility of it as one of life's pleasures. She told him she refused to be driven toward despair and have her thoughts paralyzed or defeated simply because she did not compose a cracker-jack sentence as soon as she sat down at her writing desk. She told him her work was never finished, only abandoned, then submitted.

"Maggie was right," she said, on the beach that day. "Make voyages and understand that daring, serious daring—of having the courage to pursue your dreams—lives inside of a person and is the difference between living and existing."

On the practice range the following morning, William took time away from his warm up to notice a young kid hitting balls with clubs too big for him; he saw himself in that kid, and felt a calm settle into him as he walked to the first tee.

That day William bogeyed the first three holes he played before making birdies on numbers four, five and six, two with putts of more than twenty feet. A bogey from the sand on eight left him plus one after nine holes. Considering, it was better than he expected. On the back nine, William got it up and down on number ten for par, but bogeyed the next three holes. He missed a short birdie on fourteen, but made a nice save for par on the next, a difficult par three, before making birdies at sixteen and seventeen. A par on the tough eighteenth would put him at two over for the day.

William drove his ball through the dogleg of the par four, where it came to rest behind a cluster of oak trees. He had a decent lie, and knew it would take at least a five iron to get the ball to the front edge of the putting green, much less to the pin on the second level. He had a choice of either punching out to the hundred-yard mark or trying a riskier shot over the trees, but figured he needed to post a score of four on the hole to be in contention. Let it go, he thought. He hit the shot left of where he wanted and as it lifted from the ground watched it clip several leaves that fell aimlessly downward.

He lost sight of the ball until he spotted it hitting in front of the green and rolling to the back edge, some thirty feet from the hole. He had putted well all day and made another good effort with his first putt, then tapping in for par. The score of seventy-four won him the fourth and final qualifying spot by a shot. He had shown up and made it through. He had had a bit of luck, and had somehow moved on. In a couple of months he would see another Paul Sullivan course, this time in the heart of Fort Worth, along the Trinity River.

****

To Maggie O'Connor
Late April
Star, Texas

This time I did not forget your bracelet or my rule book, and without wanting to sound anything except humble, I performed pretty well, shooting a 74 and qualifying again for the state amateur. This year's event will be held at The Llewellyn Golf Club in Fort Worth. Of course, I'll let you know how I do, but one thing is certain–I do not plan to overcook my emotions this time around.

Before the round, I saw this kid–he looked small for his age, but my guess he was not more than eleven years old–hitting balls on the practice tee. His blonde hair stuck out in all directions from his worn and faded cap, and his face was so fresh. His clubs were full-sized and too long for him, and his bag was almost as big as he was when he pulled it onto his shoulders. Later, I saw him playing by himself and every step looked to be a challenge, but we both know that was not the truth. Every step was the picture of pure joy and concentration.

"How'd you play?" William asked, noticing the youngster marking his score on the last green while practicing his own putting.

"Okay. I kind of got a bad start, but I made pars on the last four holes."

"That's good."
"Yeah," he said, smiling.

I forgot to tell you about one part of the trip to New York, the ferry ride to Ellis Island. I'd read where it had been renovated several years ago and as things worked out, decided to go there at the last second. The boat travels within a hundred yards of the Statue of Liberty before it drops passengers off onto the island. There, I walked about this amazing place and among the footsteps of so many others. It is easy to sense the hope where thousands began anew, where those with only the bundles on their backs sought the opportunity to build new lives in a strange new world.

The trees were golden and the water choppy that day. It had rained earlier and on the ride back a rainbow hung across New York harbor. I stood there taking it all in when I suddenly discovered the most precocious fourth grader beside me.

"Hey mister," he said.

"Yes," William said, turning toward the youngster with the deeply-set brown eyes and short hair.

"Can you name the colors of the rainbow in order without looking at them?"

"You know, I don't believe I can. What about you?"

"Yeah, we studied all about it in school."

"OK, then."

"Red, orange, yellow, green, blue, indigo and violet."

"Hey, that's pretty good."

"Want to know something else?"

"Sure."

The boy took a pen and paper out of his pocket. On it, he drew six separate arcs across the page and beginning from top to bottom labeled them with the colors of the rainbow.

"Red and yellow mixed together make orange," he said, pointing to the second arc. "Blue and yellow mixed together make the color green." He pointed to the fourth arc. "Violet and blue mixed together make indigo," he said, laying the point of his pencil on the sixth arc. "Some of the colors stand alone, but they also work together."

"Impressive. I never knew that."

"Do you know what DNA stands for," he asked, his eyes possessing a serious flavor.

"I know what it is, but the scientific name escapes me."

He told me, and then I asked him what the baseball term RBI meant. Not knowing created the most puzzling look on his face.

"Harry, there you are," a woman said, coming up to the boy and grabbing his hand. "I've been looking all over for you. I was worried sick."

"Yes, Mamma," he said, being pulled away. He glanced back over his shoulder at William. "See you, Mister."

"See you, Harry."

Was it George Bernard Shaw who said, "Youth is a wonderful thing, too bad it has to be wasted on children?" Surely you could argue both sides of that statement, but when I think of that small boy in Texas with the blonde hair and the big bag and the joy in his heart, and then I look back at the face of that smart child on the boat in New York–I shake my head with amazement. Two innocents whose interests I suspect are as different as night and day, will be young men soon. What will become of them?

****

For the next six weeks William was diligent in his practice sessions, but worked in more playing time, too. Most mornings and into the afternoon he attended to business interests, pondered the future, especially how it applied to the law, and read books. There was some regrouping to do on all fronts. Later in the afternoon his attention turned to golf, where he primarily worked on his putting and wedge game, then played, generally no more than six holes at a time.

Occasionally he played with friends, but primarily he stayed focused upon the task ahead in Fort Worth. He wanted to give it his best, yet he was reconciled to the fact he would never play as well as he would like, all the time considering the aftermath–playing the game solely for its own pleasure and working his way toward his final competitive swing.

June was a hot month in Fort Worth. William played only one practice round, and stayed at a place away from the course. He checked in, reviewed his yardage book and planned to play with far less internal hoopla than the previous year. He was determined not to be intimidated by his surroundings and was not. Still, a new place can toss a curve ball or two. He registered and the pairing sheets showed him going off at 7:45 a.m. the first day and 12:30 p.m. the second. I'm a better player now, he thought.

The teeing area on the starting hole was high above the fairway and in the Paul Sullivan tradition presented the player with the opportunity for a good start. Later holes would not be so generous. Number one was a slight dogleg to the left, with a wide fairway framed by deep Bermuda rough and mature pecan and mesquite trees. A prevailing south wind blew into the player's face. The green, like all the ones at The Llewellyn Golf Club, was large and sloped back to front. On the first shot of the tournament, William hit a solid driver into the fairway but pulled his second, an eight iron, slightly into the left bunker.

"I've hit this shot a thousand times," he said, addressing the ball for a shot of about fifteen yards. "Make sure the right hand comes through, keep the head quiet and do not hurry the shot–trust it and let it go."
The ball came out softly and rolled to within six feet of the cup. William was confident as he went through his routine and struck a solid putt that ran slightly through the intended break, spinning out

of the cup. He tapped in for a bogey five, and knew he had done all he could with each shot. He could live with that fact all day long.

As he walked off the green and up a slight incline to the teeing area of the next hole, a straightaway par three, William was at ease but knew he had to perform better. He had plenty of shots left. As he selected his club and addressed his ball, he reminded himself to stay in the present, that each shot stood alone. He made a good strike and the shot landed in the middle of the green. Two putts later he had made his first par.

"Par is good," he said. "Now if I can get through the horseshoe without incident, I'll be happy."

The U-shaped horseshoe at Llewellyn, the oldest of all the Sullivan-built courses, consisted of holes number three, four, and five, and playing them in even par or better was one key to having a good round. The sides of the "shoe" were challenging par fours, while the bottom part was a long and dastardly par three. All three combined to frame the practice facility which lay in the middle section.

The architect had made sure he got the attention of the player early in the game, and his uncompromising theory of traditional and challenging design and of having the public accept his concept was mirrored by the layout of the Llewellyn Golf Club. Paul Sullivan thought playing well here would be an inspiration and boost the human spirit.

Designing well-known golf courses was a far cry from the days when the architect attended public schools in Chicago and later, at age seventeen, studied journalism at Northwestern. There the tall, blue-eyed Irishman ran on the track team, edited the school paper and gained a reputation as a somewhat idealistic figure with an independent streak. That side of him surfaced quickly while studying at Oxford, where he became infatuated by the golf courses of Britain, Scotland and Ireland.

"After that, I had about as much desire to be a newspaper man as I did a farmer," he said. "I was obsessed with the idea of design and it was no use pursuing any other profession."

He brought his ideas and creations back to America. They were ones that hugged the earth of the prairies and southwest, and were based upon a simplicity and clarity of vision. But that vision was not always popular and in the early stages he constantly battled for clients and financial backers for his projects.

The Sullivan approach combined the European links-style with American traditions, and used natural landscapes–grasses, trees, rivers and wildlife–to the fullest. The architect became known for his tight and uneven fairways, holes that demanded the player shape shots, and above all, illustrate a unique skill around the greens.

Paul Sullivan was a driven man, keen of mind and blessed with the power of persuasion. He worked long hours, endured several failed marriages and eventually set down his ideas and visions to rave reviews, first in America's heartland, then in Texas and other areas of the Southwest.

"I can get things done while others are thinking about it," he said.

The son of a grocer and seamstress, both immigrants, Paul Sullivan remained faithful to his heritage, ultimately building public courses in Wisconsin and his native Illinois. There were also, besides The Llewellyn Golf Club, the exclusive ones too: Shining Bow in Tulsa, Red Hawk in Phoenix, and, of course, the San Antonio Athletic Club in southern Texas.

William knew he had to hit more of a slinging-type of hook to contend with the severe dogleg of the third hole. Hitting it too straight would send the ball through the fairway and into the rough on the right. Hooking it too quickly offered the player no shot whatsoever from the grove of pecans that grew along the left side. Still the player must hit the tee ball far enough to carry the three large fairway bunkers at the neck of the severe dogleg. It was a shot that required power, accuracy and execution, and was the key play on the hole.

"Get over," he said, as he watched his first shot leave the club. The contact was square and the trajectory good, but the ball did not bend enough in the air, and William knew it would travel through the fairway and come to rest in the right rough. The ball nestled down in the Bermuda grass; problem enough, but the main obstacle was a thick tree limb full of branches that prevented him from hitting a full shot of any kind. William hit a low punch shot short of the green that hopped up, gathered speed, and ended up on the downslope behind the green. He pitched nicely to four feet and made the putt.

"Better," he said, pulling the ball out of the cup and moving on.

William selected a four wood on the teeing ground of the long par three. He worried about getting the ball over the deep sand bunkers that guarded the front of the green and in doing so, failed to make a quality swing. The ball came off the club weakly and ended up short and to the right. From there he made sure his pitch shot carried onto the putting surface, where he two putted for a bogey. Still, he managed to get what he could from the situation.

The concluding hole of the horseshoe ran alongside the Trinity River on the right and a solid line of pecan and mesquites to the left. The hole was long, and curved slightly to the right while the fairway sloped left.

"This is a monster," William said, taking a deep breath before sticking his wooden tee into the ground.

William decided to take his first chance of the round and chose to play driver while one playing partner hit a three wood and the other a one iron. Both balls landed safely in the fairway, but the pair faced second shots of more than two hundred and twenty yards. William's tee shot paralleled the river on a high trajectory and curved back to the left, landing further down the fairway.

"Best shot of the day," he said, walking toward his ball. "Sometimes, I actually believe I can do this."

Pars at five, six, seven and eight left him at plus two going to number nine, a par five that ran downwind and presented what he thought ought to be a birdie opportunity. One over par would be okay, he thought, but that sort of thinking went to the future and his tee shot veered right instead of turning left, landing in the water hazard. Par now became his best score and more than likely he was looking at bogey or more. He felt stupid for the slip, and nothing affected him more than thinking poorly.

"Hitting a bad shot happens," he said, scolding himself. "But concentration and being focused is one of the few things I can control out here."

The lateral hazard his tee shot found was situated in such a way that dropping the ball on the left of it presented William with a long and obstructed shot. But the rules also permitted the player to drop the ball on the opposite side of a hazard, if it was an equal distance from the hole and of no advantage to the player. From there William lofted the ball over the trees and down the fairway, leaving only a seven-iron shot to the green and an outside chance at par. He did not make the score intended, but he did minimize the mistake with a bogey six.

"That's pretty cool," he said. "Good execution, being dumb, smart and creative—all on the same hole."

At the turn, his spirits were lifted, his head held high. The course suited his eye. He liked it and had found a temporary comfort zone. Like a tailor, he was stitching together a good round as he stepped onto the tenth tee, a downhill par three. He selected a six iron in order to get the ball near the pin on the back of the green. The solid shot landed about ten feet back of the flag but his putt broke more to the left than he anticipated and William tapped in for par. He knew a player had to make putts if he was going to score well; however, all he could do was bring a positive attitude and some relaxation to the stroke. Coupled with some technique, those were the basic requirements.

William hit his best drives of the day on the next two holes. He made his first birdie of the day on eleven but three-putted from eighteen feet on twelve for bogey. He had wrapped his attention in an eagerness to make the putt and climb closer to even par but sailed it five feet by and missed it again coming back.

"Horrible, horrible mistake," he said aloud, feeling a bit downtrodden. He could not quite figure things out about this game—the player had to possess confidence, yet cockiness often yielded humbling situations and unexpected outcomes. The game could grab you by the scruff of the neck just when you felt the best.

He missed the fairway and green on both thirteen and fourteen, failing to get the ball up and down on either occasion. "Seventy-five is better than seventy-six," he said.

William finished exactly there, shooting a first-round score of seventy-five and chances were, if he repeated the performance tomorrow and tradition was any measure, he had a chance to play on the weekend. The round was a good one for him—he was not a long hitter, but kept the driver in play most of the day, putted fairly well and for the most part stuck to his guns of aggressive execution and a conservative strategy.

As he walked to the practice tee to work on his long and short game, the idea he fought and scrapped and had gotten about what he could out of his round struck him as a positive note; it struck his fancy, too. He was tired but uplifted and would do no more than an hour's work in order to prepare for tomorrow. Thoughts of Jane Parker hit him—he had not forgotten her completely, and for a moment he tried to imagine what she might be doing and how good it might feel to share his joy with her. It was strange. He had not wallowed in his mistake with the woman, but he had gotten in the habit of being aware of it by thinking of her, of sensing the loss and just when he could not quite bear the idea another moment, taking it just one step further. He figured everyone had their way of learning and at least for now, this was his.

The scoreboard had him eight shots behind the leader, but he did not care about that; his goal was a much humbler one. "I have to take care of my end," he said to himself.

The following day, William came to the par three fifteenth hole three over par, one shot better than in the previous round. He was in a decent position to survive the cut if he could hang on and post a number of at least 150. He had been successful so far by being tension-free, paying attention to each shot, and holding onto his concentration; of just playing the game. The hole measured 166 yards to the middle of the green, but a twenty mph breeze directly behind him made his club selection a bit trickier. The Trinity River guarded the hole in the front and sand bunkers on the remaining three sides, so choosing the right club was the first hurdle, hitting the ball solidly and on line the next. Par was indeed a good score.

He had played well enough today and was fighting hard–that mattered. He struck the shot solidly and it sailed high and on target. "Be good," one of his fellow competitors said. The ball hit in the middle of the green but bounded long, missing the back bunker and sliding down an embankment behind the green. He pitched up and two putted from fifteen feet, and had to be satisfied with the bogey. Last year, he might have taken an unnecessary chance and made a five or six rather than four. Today, he took his medicine.

The par five sixteenth was reachable in two for him, but he made a poor swing on his second shot, a three wood from the left side of the fairway. The ball came to rest in a grass bunker sixty yards away from its intended destination and his third shot left him with a twenty-foot putt that lipped out of the hole. He did everything he could do with the ball and it just did not go in. On seventeen, William drove it into the fairway and wedged to twelve feet, but missed to the right. He tapped in for four, and figured he needed a par or better on the final hole, a long par four playing into the wind.

On the final hole, William hooked his tee ball and it struck a huge pecan tree, again on the left–dropping straight down into the rough. A three wood and a pitch shot to within ten feet of the hole gave him a chance. As he studied the putt William turned his senses toward putts he had made. He figured that was the attitude he trained himself to employ at this moment. Take dead aim, he told himself as he looked at the hole and back at his ball. When he looked up the ball curved right slightly and found the center of the hole. A second-round score of seventy-five left him exactly where he wanted to be.

"I'm happy that I gave myself a chance," he said.

William was relieved as he took off his cap and shook hands with his fellow competitors. He would wait for the news.

"Nothing better than doing your best," he said softly, welcoming the other side of life to kick in. "It's like walking on air."

5

William decided to spend the night at Fairway Farms after the tournament scoreboard confirmed he would not play Saturday and Sunday. The drive there was far different than a year ago, when his mind's eye did not comprehend the beauty of the countryside he passed or relish the competition just undertaken.

Despite the heat but because of the spring rains, the flowers still bloomed and the prickly pear cactus, with its red and yellow blossoms, blended in with the high grasses in the fields and on the hillsides. He drove on a state highway that traveled past limestone cliffs and ledges, crossed bridges and the rivers that ran quickly below them. In the winter, he had seen the limestone white with snow and the bridges iced over, but today the Texas sky was high and blue, the wind hot. Cattle, horses and sheep grazed in the pastures, and the silver wings of several windmills, broken and bent, crept along as they instinctively sought the wind. This was rural Texas and the way home.

In the back pastures of his mind, William's heartbeat signaled thumbs up, despite the fact he would miss the final two rounds of the tournament. The recorded voices of Sinatra, Delbert McClinton, Springsteen, and the cool jazz of Miles Davis and Bill Evans filled the vacuum in which he lived; the melodies poured out of them and he inhaled their songs.

"How good is this?" he asked.

He passed bike racers in training, their sleek machines peddled by men and women with lean bodies wearing helmets and uniforms of bright colors. He admired their determination as they spun into a slight headwind, their spines straight, their legs pumping, and resolve written on their collective faces. As they mowed down the miles, they rode single file within inches of one another at an astonishing pace.

About ten miles outside Calahan he took what some locals believed to be a short cut, a dirt road that led the traveler into the past. The Old Union Road as it was called was more of a graded ranch road than anything else, and barely wide enough for two vehicles to pass one another. The road curved along a dry creek bed, with stands of cottonwoods, a hilly landscape of cedar and yellow flowers, and crossed two narrow wooden bridges built during the Depression years. The road was not taken much except for those who lived off it and maybe the postmaster and an occasional UPS truck. William liked the stone walls built when Texas was referred to as a Republic, the character of the crippled fence posts, and the land, most of which was farmed or ranched. The old road stretched for several miles and connected the old and new.

A half hour later he pulled the car into the driveway at Fairway Farms. It was late afternoon but evening lay around the corner. When he arrived, Maria came out of the house to greet him. She had a basket filled with cut flowers she planned to make into several arrangements. Hector was at the feed store. William went upstairs to shower, but before going back downstairs went into Maggie's room, and standing beside her desk looked out the window onto the gardens, just as he had done the very first time he had visited the room. The garden below looked as peaceful as ever, fresh. He was as calm at that instant as any time in his life; a serenity that had been fought for and won, at least temporarily.

Later in the lower garden, he tried to let things settle in and settle down as he sat in his favorite chair and sipped a whiskey; the crystal glass heavy and strong in his hand. On occasion, he would look up and notice things, and listen to the sounds of the day. The wind rattled the gate to the preserve and he wondered what he would say to Maggie about the tournament, among other things.

****

To Maggie O'Connor
Summertime
Fairway Farms

At the beginning of the second round on Friday I was a jangle of nerves. Same old story I guess–not that confident in my ability, hoping rather than expecting to do well, wanting something too badly, trying to be too perfect, not trusting myself enough–same book, different cover. Then a strange thing happened after my shot on the second hole–what I had been working on all these months suddenly clicked into being. Of course, I do not dare claim it will last, because I know there still can be bad patches where confusion, a lost swing and too many voices take the player in a tight, downward spiral.

Click: Be athletic and pay attention–to the target.

Click: Be faithful to the pre-shot routine and if necessary, one swing thought.

Click: Spend less time over the ball and trust in the practice.

Click: Let the shot go wherever it wants, caring less about the result.

Click: Be determined, but patient enough to let the game come to you.

Click: Play each shot with conviction and a concentrated mind.

Conviction, that's the ticket that passed me through to the other side.

The fact that I began playing from my heart became an energizing and positive thing. It did not guarantee I would hit every shot perfectly because I did not, but it certainly focused my efforts on playing the game, of making the best score on every hole that I could. And it was much more fun.

Suddenly I addressed shots with a turned up collar and a different composition to my attitude, subconsciously saying, "Boys, I'm here to play, kick your collective butts and not concede a thing." There are a number of things inherent to the game of golf, but whining is not one of them. I can now join the game rather than endlessly chase my tail—what a relief that is.

Back to the golf; today I made par on the three tough holes that comprised the horseshoe and played three-over-par golf until I missed a couple of opportunities on the back nine. Still after the best save of either round on eighteen and a two-day total of 150, I figured I was in good shape. Well, I was half right.

That is until I reached to retrieve my ball after the final putt and noticed something that almost instantly sickened me. It was not my ball. It was the same brand name and number, but missing was my small black identification mark. I turned it in my fingers to make sure as I stood there on the green, but for the life of me I could not find my mark. Had it been rubbed off somehow? The fact was I had not holed out with the ball I had struck from the teeing ground.

I thought: No one would ever know about this. Then I thought: I would. In the larger world it may mean nothing but it sure meant something to me. I was momentarily saddened by the discovery, but uplifted that I knew the rule and recognized what must be done, regardless of the consequences.

There are rules and rules govern play. It was similar to the law and in some ways, to the way our beliefs help us conduct our lives. Someone brought that to my attention not too long ago.

So prior to leaving the green (as you know I would have been disqualified if I had walked off) I informed my fellow-competitors and the rules official of the infraction, and proceeded back down the fairway toward the pecan tree with hope that I would recover my original ball. If not, I knew I'd have to return to the teeing ground and play another ball with an added penalty of stroke and distance in addition to the two-shot penalty I had already incurred for playing the wrong ball.

Long story short—I found my original ball about ten paces from the tree and proceeded to make par, however, the six now on my card moved the two-day total to 152, two strokes off the eventual cut line. Later, several players approached and congratulated me, but deep down I likened it to the day Bobby Jones called a penalty on himself that ultimately cost him a national championship. "You might as well praise a man for not robbing a bank," he said.

I miss playing this weekend, but there is a strong sense of redemption roaming around inside of me this afternoon; peace too. I took a voyage and even though it did not turn out exactly as I wished, I've accomplished what asked to do—I failed better. Sometimes the past has nothing to do with the present. The way I figure it, the truth has value, but no price.

William sat there quietly in the lower garden. He wanted to say more, but simply laid down his pen. He could have gone inside or returned to Star, but he decided to ride the day out into the darkness and think about what lay ahead.

"Who in the world is it?" he asked.

"I don't know William, she didn't say," Maria said, handing him the phone.

"Hello."

"William, its Jane. Jane Parker."

"Jane, are you okay? Where are you?"

"I'm back in New York. Things did not work out in England. It took me awhile to realize it, but I guess my heart was somewhere else."

"Really?"

"Really."

"There is a place I'd like you to see," he said. "If it is okay with you, I'd like to make the arrangements?"

"Yes, it's quite okay with me."

They spoke awhile longer before William set the phone down and leaned back in the chair. He sighed deeply and closed his eyes. Suddenly the golf tournament and everything prior to the conversation were in the distance, growing smaller.

When he opened his eyes a few moments later they were cast skyward. It was a clear day except for the pale yellow orb sitting halfway above the horizon in the East. From where he sat in the lower garden, the moon looked as if it were balancing on the pitch of the rooftop, rising. A mockingbird landed on the roof, almost directly between William and the moon, his singing voice as pure and confident as any William had ever heard. It was the second time in a year he had seen the moon in the late afternoon. This time it was full and looked like it hung from an invisible wire in the sky. Then again, he had only been looking up for a short time. As darkness arrived, and the stars began to appear in the sky, they shone brighter than ever, as if someone had polished and wiped them clean.

6

Some Time Later

To Maggie O'Connor
Autumn
Fairway Farms

Telegram: Keys to the First Ball

Near the conclusion of your original letter to me you wrote, "A player can never hit the second ball first because the conditions have changed prior to striking it, and conditions determine play. The player has more information and less fear, hence it is like picking the lotto numbers on Sunday morning. Now, the keys to not missing the first one—that is an entirely different matter."

In golf, this is often referred to as the rub of the green or playing as it lays, but you know and I know—the first ball is not just about golf. Gradually, I have learned that focusing upon hitting the first ball is where the path to mastery begins, but more importantly, that finding and understanding the keys in that particular journey lies in a far different place and is a great deal more challenging than I originally expected.

Of course time has passed and some experience has been gained during the last couple of years, but your presence never fades; not because of golf necessarily although the sport connected us, but due to the fact you helped steer my thinking in a different direction; toward what I believed, who I had become, and where I might be going. You asked that I consider remodeling and relying upon my heart and soul, that I dare to trust them and march in tandem with them into the world, regardless of the task at hand. You have been an angel on my shoulder, a nudge to my conscience and consciousness, and for some reason noticed something in me that I did not know existed. My friend Jane Parker said as much on several occasions, but one tends to dismiss those types of comments, especially when they deceive themselves into thinking they are all powerful and wise. I'm feeling lucky I guess because only few of us get another crack, a second chance.

It is possible the seeds of rethinking and reshaping my life were planted already; otherwise I might not have left San Francisco and the positive things I had accomplished there. I loved the law and my future was bright in many ways, but something inside of me suggested I needed more—or at least different. I suspect we all have these inklings from time to time. The mystery lies in how to act upon them.

One of the many things golf taught me was that a player must, at some point, give up control in order to gain control. It was a difficult lesson to learn, perhaps even more difficult to implement, since our tendencies as human beings are geared more in the opposite direction. This endless journey would have never gotten off the ground without your generous response to my letter and the fact that you believed in the power of ideas and ideals, convictions, and the obligation to follow them through. My wish is that I never lose sight of the words you left for me. They represent a truth, a complete and relentless honesty I do not intend to abandon.

Like you, I carry those words written for Lord Byron by Tennessee Williams around with me:

"Lately I've been listening to hired musicians behind a row of artificial palm trees instead of the single pure instrument of my heart. For what is the heart, but an instrument that turns chaos into order, noise into music. Make voyages, attempt them. There is nothing else."

In golf (and life), timing is everything, and I've discovered that when a voyage begins the passenger might know where he will end up, but not what will occur along the way. I've learned to welcome those surprises and that to do so, one must believe in themselves.

There have been times the last couple of years when I have met defeat and plowed on, and if the truth be known, when I have flinched and given ground. What few things I achieved were off to the side, and I was happier there. For the longest, I was forlorn with that fact, because I understood the badge of courage belongs to the one who can break and come back stronger than ever before. Have I done that to my satisfaction? Probably not.

Still, I found that I liked to practice less and play more, to leave more to the moment, the unexpected and unforeseen. Through play, I began to learn about risk, daring and the ability to be enthralled by the surprises that resulted. I found I played with happiness, fresh blood in my veins and hope on my sleeve, rhythms I had misplaced somewhere along the line. It is good to tell about things that have been overcome, don't you think?

I've learned our beliefs are subject to change. If we are learners, they constantly come under scrutiny and run into challenges. But there must be something to govern our conduct when confusion reigns or decisions and actions must be taken. I strive to be an honest man, without sentimentality—not just in the darkness and solitude of my room, but for all seasons; when the irises bloom and the leaves fall to the ground, when the park benches fill, then empty, and even when doubt and restlessness hang in the air. That is a cool thing.

So is the tolerance of others that believe and behave differently than me, yet I hope—I'd like to think—I would stand tall for my views. Reasonable people can disagree, right? Seeking and not being afraid of the truth helps with that, but I find that I have a hard time living up to those things in life that I think ought to be lived up to. Perhaps my views have changed because I had the opportunity to see things in a different light during the last several years. I have some quarrels with the South, but there is a sense of continuity here, and I think more than anything, it comes from place.

There is other news.

Some years ago I met a woman; her father was a surveyor and her mother a nurse. She was like a diamond—beautiful and brilliant—and if possible, a more precious gem today. She is a compassionate and remarkably unselfish woman who has taught me as you taught me.

We've listened to the Aspen leaves ripple in the wind on a mountainside outside of Santa Fe. We've seen the beauty of a colt kicking up his heels in the early morning while his mother, a Dun mare, looked on with pride and amusement. We've hiked on the prairie, among tall and native grasses, the bison and Black-eyed Susans; there too we've felt the light fade on our shoulders and the silence arrive at the end of the day.

We have journeyed to and explored some of our greatest cities; our oceans too, where she has taught me about the language of the sea, and how the tides and waves can replenish the heart and soul. I have learned to be present for such moments. I watch her from a distance and realize I am no longer the center of the universe–that like you told me, things continue to change within us. I have learned that showing up matters; that love and balance are gifts, and that every day counts for something. She has taught me that conversation is different from dialogue, and that listening and laughter count, big-time. You see, Jane Parker knocked on my door again and this time, I answered.

That day the sun shone through every window at Fairway Farms and the curtains were blowing in the ones which were opened; it was a radiant day. She delivered clarity, purpose, and a connection to everyday life at my doorstep; she has made each day remarkable. She has made an ordinary life extraordinary. Today, she is the song I sing, the summer rain, and the first star in the night sky all rolled into one.

We have a child–a daughter named Olivia Sarah. She too is a beautiful creature with soft blonde hair, and wide, dreamy, gray-blue eyes. Her face, with her mother's high cheekbones and expressiveness, is somewhat Asian-looking.

As with all fathers, my heart has been removed from my chest and is now a mobile heart, beating outside of my body. My hopes run from the touching to the absurd, but they are always ones wishing her an eventful and happy life.

I imagine teaching her from my grandfather's aluminum stool about golf and life, including the first ball. I hope to teach her about living appropriately and making voyages, to always make voyages. And as in golf, that life is filled with promises and possibilities.

When I teach her about golf—I will tell her about what I have learned and hope it will help her along. I will tell her to play with fury and know that a champion is made on the back practice fields when no one is watching. I will teach her that it is fine to be confident but that she will meet doubt, regardless of her ability. I will help her flourish in an environment where it is okay to care, to want to do your best, and to seek excellence. I will encourage her by letting her know if she does things to the best of her ability, she will do well (and good).

She has such bright and intense eyes and I will explain that her athletic and life compass can take her in any direction she wishes; that she has the free will to choose. That is important I think. I hope she will dream beyond what she thinks is possible, but understand balance is crucial, and that she can forgive herself for not being perfect. I will teach her that nothing is to be feared, only understood.

She likes books and will be a reader; she is curious, a learner and daring. I believe we will visit the emergency room of our hospital any day now. She loves music, nature and human beings. Her mother sees to that. For me, ours is the perfect Trinity.

We have purchased Fairway Farms; it has been our home for some time now. Our child was born here. Hector and Maria are part of our lives—Olivia plays with the twins, Isabelle and Zavalla, when they come to visit, and I believe you would be pleased by the laughter and young voices. Elizabeth Nathan first held out the idea and I asked Hector and Maria what they would think. Everyone agreed—you would approve. I hope you are smiling.

The gardens are as prosperous as ever—the colors, smells and songbirds working overtime. On the porch we have a basket of apples, some pumpkins and several pots of herbs mingling with the scents of the pines and flora. Our family walks in the preserve often. There are some wild fig trees that have sprung up in the thistle, just past the gate. It is amazing how nature overcomes its differences.

Soon I will seek the definition of estuary or understand more of the Sand Hill Cranes that fly over, their fluttering cries and long lean bodies small from my perspective on earth. Are they coming or going from the Platte River in Nebraska? It is up to me to anticipate such questions, to find the answers, and to have the curiosity to seek them out. Olivia will see to that.

We fish in the pond and use the wooden boat to travel around to the coves and marshes. I like that Olivia enjoys the music of nature; that she simply loves these types of things. The blackbird still nests in the spine of the yucca and the sounds of the old owl, doves and quail travel the countryside. Several red-tail hawks glide and climb overhead, always hunting. Olivia likes to watch the turtles sunning themselves, listen to the frogs bark at night and is amused by the ovals in the water created when the fish school. She laughs and asks a million questions, in her own way. She looks up too, and watches the stars. She does not think about luck or getting angry; she always has a good day. I think that is extraordinary.

Your room is the same as you left it except for some slight alterations. Jane uses your desk by the window as her writing table and comments daily about something she sees while working. It fits her and I thought you'd appreciate it is a place being put to good use. It is her study, the room of one's own most of us need.

I do have a confession to make and it is a result of sitting at your desk alone one evening while Jane was out of town. I was rumbling and rummaging around all anxious and excited about the days ahead. That night I found a journal of yours stored in a side panel of the desk, its paper a bit yellow and worn and the back still strong. Time had been spent there and I read some of the things you wrote about my grandfather. I did not go too far with the invasion, but some of your words led to new insights; others resurrected memories of the man that raised me. When done, I returned it to the place it belongs.

"William Polk Bradford died today and I was fortunate enough to know him," the passage began. "He was a fine human being–warm, unselfish, blessed with character and judgment, and the courage of his conviction. He was a courtly and sophisticated man, indeed charming; a man of the South who grew to age in a part of the country that was adapted to boyhood, and produced a man with a gentle manner and without personal venom.

"I liked his penetrating blue eyes and his ruddy, handsome face from the start, but his spirit most of all. He was graceful in his demeanor and conversation. He had a journalist's mind, active and always playing with different subjects. He liked a big breakfast and he enjoyed cooking suppers of chili, steaks, and tamales for a small gathering of friends. He drank bourbon when outside and scotch indoors.

"He was an excellent fly fisherman, a better than average painter and once a first-rate boxer and golfer. He was a reader, a lover of books, words and ideas. I think mainly because he grew up in a home where his father quoted poetry, and asked his children questions about history and current affairs at the dinner table.

"He never remarried, but raised a grandson that made him proud. He told him to run straight in life and to see potential trouble in seeking power at all costs. He was proud of young William's legal footwork because it showed qualities of hard work, attention, and that he understood there was no short cut.

"William Polk Bradford kept an open mind, especially about me. For that I am grateful; he was one of my best friends. Throughout most of my life I've remained unwaveringly loyal to the principle of looking forward, but at times like these, I glance back over my shoulder at one of the threads of life that ultimately determine who we are."

I have always thought that sometimes when we look back our thoughts and remembrances are more selective than truthful, but in the case of my grandfather I think you hit the nail on the head. I suppose my grandfather knew that one day age would trump his desire, even mock it. He always told me that shame was one of the main reasons great players left the game. But in all the hours he spent with me he never did anything except encourage me to keep my eyes on the stars and my feet on the ground; advice that I lost temporarily and recently found. I look in the mirror these days and swear I see a face that more and more resembles my grandfather's. I see his hands in my hands. I noticed them the other day while carrying Olivia to her room after she had fallen asleep downstairs. These are the hands that caught my fall as a toddler, gripped the leather of a golf club, tied shoelaces, wrote letters, shook the hands of strangers, and consoled friends. They are the hands that have sweated in labor, trembled in nervousness and anger. They reflect a life lived, and they are more wrinkled, bent, and rugged now.

Jane Parker is the smartest person I know.

She follows a strict regime in regards to her work and writes in her study (at your desk) from 9 a.m.-2 p.m. every day, producing about fifteen-hundred words. During these times she is steady, but not that talkative and a bit forgetful. She seldom takes a day off while working on a project.

As of today, she has sold less of her fiction than she would like, and takes the attitude it is simply not good enough, that the projects completed so far serve as an apprenticeship. She seeks to get better, and compares it to Olivia crawling before she could walk. She has told me that she views writing as an act of faith, resulting from years of living, study and reading.

"The story will be around forever," she said. "And it is the story that counts, above all else."

"But how do you know what the story is?" I asked.

"We all have a thousand stories in us. It is the one that makes a dent and tugs at you in some way that becomes your subject."

Like me, she is a solitary soul living an unpredictable and challenging life in her study each day. It must be hard and she admits to that, but seldom discusses it with me. I know that she is a passionate spirit, a truth seeker whom I love and respect apart from her work.

There is some sad news to report.

In yesterday's sports section of the San Antonio paper there was a good-size write-up of a man we both knew, Tank Cotton. There were several photographs of him, most as the well-known caddie and caddie master that worked at the San Antonio Athletic Club for more than forty years. There was one with that great group of Texans–Hogan, Nelson, Burke, Demaret, and Ransom; and another of you Maggie, when he looped for you during your march to a major championship.

"Joseph Douglass 'Tank' Cotton died quietly on Monday, in peace and dignity," the article said.

The obituary also spoke of his friendship with Dr. Martin Luther King Jr. and how in his own way he fought what was called "the starless midnight of racism" in Texas and other places in the South. There were many on the record comments and it is clear he was a symbol of human dignity.

I think I told you I ran into him following my disastrous first round that year.

"How'd you do, champ?" he asked.

"Not too well I'm afraid, the rain flustered me. Unlucky I guess."

"Can I say something?" he asked

"Sure."

"When you get back home and one day pull back the curtains to find a driving rain outside–put yourself out there and play in the poor weather and prepare for these types of conditions. On a day like today, with the wind and rain–more than half the players in the field are beaten before they ever strike a ball.

"Be a gamer–battle and grind to the end, despite the conditions," he said that day, holding out his hand. I thanked him.

I do not know if Tank Cotton had a lot of money or not, but by almost all accounts at the root of his civil rights convictions was a profound faith in the basic goodness of folks; a belief that in my eyes made him a rich man. I thought you ought to know of his outcome.

My search for the keys to the first ball has taken me in unexpected and challenging directions since returning to Texas. I do not play the game competitively any longer, but solely for its own pleasure. It is the way it should be and not a way of life, which it became briefly. My fling, however, was worthwhile; it delivered balance and love. Ending competitive play does not mean I do not take the game seriously.

But it is Jane and Olivia who come first now, then my profession—the law—and finally, golf. It is still a challenging feat to hit a stationary ball with a stick the proper distance and in the right direction. It is a frustrating and humorous game, one that whether we are a professional, amateur, or one that plays infrequently, hoodwinks us into thinking we will play well. It has taken industry and a bit of luck on my part, but I have rediscovered its joys, even though I seldom take part.

Golf is both science and art. Through your teaching and guidance I've learned to remain in the present and pay attention. I've learned that errant shots are inevitable, but to dismiss them quickly and attempt to focus upon the good ones. I've learned about being positive in the eyes of failure, to let go and always attempt to fail better. I've learned that trust is a fundamental requirement, that practice is a necessity, that process leads one in all sorts of directions, and seeking excellence and doing your best is a good thing, a higher calling. I believe that.

But I've learned too that golf is not a simple game—it requires stamina, patience, an inner flame, and a belief that the answer is out there, regardless of the problem at hand. I've learned success does not come easily, and that the game has the potential to inflict upon a player everything from silliness to shame and defeat. It also demands mammoth determination and coolness in the face of the odds. The game is best played with passion and not anger, because one will serve you well, the other will not. As you have said many times, golf is the most fickle of games and one that can only be joined and not conquered. I've learned I have the will to win; I've learned that will is part of talent; I've learned having it allows a player to give it their all, regardless of the circumstances. There is an obligation to be mindful of these things.

As the days wore on, William Scott Bradford never returned to tournament golf and in fact rarely played. He did, however, stay connected to the game that had taught him so much about life. Early each morning he hit about fifty balls, usually with a seven iron, from the same mat and location Maggie used when she lived at Fairway Farms. The pattern of the balls, either in the air or when they landed on the ground some one hundred forty yards away, was not nearly as precise as that of his former teacher. When done, William walked out into the seventh fairway and picked up the balls, sometimes with Olivia in tow, often waving to the course ranger parked on a hill nearby.

"Do you think the comment, look for the moon in the afternoon because that is when its existence is most in doubt, has merit?" Maggie had asked in their first meeting.

Since those original exchanges, William came to realize that Maggie's question had more to do with hope, courage and daring in life than anything else. He knew to implement these ideas and ideals was a process that did not take shape overnight and required not only a professed belief, but a commitment of direct action, even if it meant failure or disappointment. The voyages she spoke of were not geographical journeys or reckless adventures, but travels of the imagination, heart and soul; the serious daring a state of mind, a belief one can take anywhere in the world. He figured that attempting to find the moon in the afternoon was about the best of our humanity.

William believed embedded into the basic human condition was the need to dream, to try and often to fail; to hope against hope, to sail into the wind, and to believe passionately in something. He believed one could leap any wall with a heart constructed in this manner, but he knew, too, few paid close enough attention. He believed in chasing that potential, and character ultimately mattered. It represented one's true currency and passport.

In many ways, William had become a fatalist and was fond of saying his horizon, where advanced planning was concern, extended only a couple of weeks. He often wondered how Olivia would remember him. He hoped less as a lawyer (he had closed the door completely on returning to the law-firm partnership in San Francisco) and more of a teacher (he traveled to Austin twice a week to head law classes at the university). But more importantly, as a man who gave love without demanding it be returned, and as a man who had the courage to confront his weaknesses.

Jane's outlook had more of an edge to it. She was not inhibited or intimidated by conventional wisdom, and she thought about her positions constantly, always seeking innovative ways to look around the corner or to pull the curtain open, even wider. Deeply set inside her was devotion to clarity and precision and the unending battle of becoming a writer. She had faith but often expressed disaffection with religion, one of many subjects about the national soul she probed in her stories. Her work had an unaffected style and addressed universal themes, and often her characters lived ordinary lives. Through them she attempted to reveal lives that were frequently invisible to others. It was the strongest component of her writing.

She believed that out of emotion came form. She believed in hard work, exercise and voting, and behind closed doors she was a prankster who transformed those around her with a hearty enjoyment of life. Her golden brown hair had a touch of pearl gray in it now and her family mattered more than her literary career, but there was that, too. Jane remained a woman who refused to narrow her horizon or turn her face away from the sea. She was a woman who would not narrow her horizon or turn her face away from the sea.

But she loved William, always had. Sometimes he wondered why, how these two hearts blended together. He figured some luck was involved, and that many questions simply do not have nice, neat answers. What he knew about her and love was she had been hurt a time or two and had a good sense of what that meant to others. The pair did not live inside one another's pockets, but together they had learned to sustain a certain level of intensity that balance and love required.

Place mattered. Jane and he discussed it a lot. They had a keen sense of Southern history, and the webs of life there. William was disheartened by the tone and content of conversations he overheard sometimes, and occasionally questioned why he had returned home. He knew the debate should and probably would last a lifetime. But there was continuity here, in this place. The keys on his ring were fewer in number today and for the most part, he knew what locks they fit. He was no longer afraid of happy endings, the truth, or following his heart; it was part of looking up.

Time mattered, yet the gardens and preserve at Fairway Farms were timeless and powerful. There were no rules; the constituents of the arbors, informal borders and sections of plants were wild with color, fragrance and diversity. The complete garden had a suitable design, but somehow gave the impression it lacked structure. It was a useful and completely trustworthy space, and a place where the traveler could read or simply walk and think. The gardens were romantic, yet practical, experimental, yet respectful of tradition and the past. It was a place that rendered pleasure every month of the year.

Jane and Olivia became amateur gardeners, but William hung his hat on the natural preserve beyond the gate. Hector taught the two gardeners they had to be resourceful and it was a discipline whose components can never be learned completely; and they would encounter problems that must be directly addressed. The amateur Jane Parker believed in the endeavor, that it challenged her intelligence and educated her. She learned, too, that gardening was not without its consequences and acceptance; of time spent, of time spent bent-over, pulling or digging and the occasional aches and pains that accompany some of those things. And Hector taught her the gardener had to have a tinge of ruthlessness—that if something did not contribute to the whole, it might have to be replaced.

Jane and Olivia learned about the seasons. About autumn, when the red leaves of the maples and oaks signaled winter approaching; when the hearty marigold, with its orange, gold and yellow varieties are called upon to provide some necessary color. About winter, when some plants are moved indoors, bulbs for spring are planted, and pansies survive the first frost. He taught them about spring, when the irises add color and elegance, and about summer, when the gardener hopes for some rain and decent blooms.

Olivia followed Maria around constantly, especially when she was cutting and gathering flowers for the vases and arrangements indoors. She taught Olivia what flowers to select, how to cut them and which to press her nose toward, taking in the fragrance.

Maria always took her basket to the garden when she selected the flowers, but she also wore an apron with a pocket across the front, just in case. Occasionally, Olivia helped pick field daisies for the jug vase, but the arrangements for the painted fox vases, the handsome porcelain vases and some others, generally set on low tables, came exclusively from the wildflower and cutting gardens. There were some tall vases, too, for the American Beauty roses and delphiniums Jane had planted. Olivia liked to water the plants in the flowerpots that came in all sizes and were arranged accordingly on the outdoor porch. The little girl liked to help, but she liked spying the hummingbirds even more.

William concentrated on the acres of the preserve; it became a room of his own he liked to share. He figured it had matured into what Maggie had envisioned–the moan of doves, fields of crimson clover and buttercups. Wild things, like the figs, thistle, pear trees or blueberries that grew close to the ground. He had built a small boat house out of cedar that had turned light gray from the seasons. Against it he planted pyracantha and hollies, their red berries, thorns and prickly edges the right fit for the preserve. In the waters, he fished for small-mouth bass, perch and brim. Olivia delivered a smile to his heart when she went with him and asked if the fish walked on their fins or mermaids might rise out of the water. The pair often searched for four-leaf clovers.

Just as for Maggie, William and Jane wanted the gardens to be part of Olivia's earliest set of memories and her childhood. They planted two trees, almonds rather than pines, outside her bedroom window and took many photographs. William especially liked the one where Olivia and her two cats, Kit and Scout, walked together along the garden path that led into the natural preserve. It reflected a spirited, often rebellious girl who had taught the pair as kittens to accompany her on her adventures. Another favorite was taken of Jane and Olivia on the bench by the camellia garden, their books and paints lying beside them. He relished the idea that Jane taught their daughter the value of a woman's skill with a pen and watercolor brush. He liked that Olivia never stopped being eager to learn, that she was full of small surprises and without even trying, enjoyed the fullness of youth.

"Daddy, what would it be like to ride on a ray of light?" she asked one day.

Sometimes when he stood at the upstairs window and looked down, he watched them in the garden–hand in hand; sometimes Olivia lagged behind because she was curious about one thing or another. Attendants Kit and Scout were never too far away. He imagined the mother-daughter conversation being intimate, light-hearted and instructive, and as always, unhurried.

THE END

About the Author

Dick Sheffield was born in Fort Worth, Texas, the son of two public school teachers. After graduating from the University of Texas at Austin and the Kennedy School of Government at Harvard, he has spent most of his career as a journalist with ABC News in New York, covering politics.

He has also been a reporter and managing editor of a small-town newspaper and served on the staffs of Senator Edward M. Kennedy, Congressman Charles Wilson and Ambassador Allard K. Lowenstein.

In 1985, he attended the Bread Loaf Writers' Conference in Middlebury, Vermont. It was 2010 when one of his short stories, Maere Tungol, was recognized as a third-prize winner by the Hackney Literary Awards, a national story competition. The Birmingham Arts Journal published the piece in 2011.

He and his wife Anita live in San Angelo, Texas, and New York City, and since 2007 he has served as a United States Golf Association committeeman (USGA).

Lasso the Moon is his first novel.

For more information,
www.dicksheffield.com

Find more books from Keith Publications, LLC At

www.wickedinkpress.com
www.dinkwell.com
www.dreamsnfantasies.com